I0621170

TAKING
A CHANCE

Part of the
Pine City Chance Series

by

Marcella DiPaolo

ISBN: 978-1-64395-009-9 (Kindle eBook)
ISBN: 978-1-64395-109-6 (Paperback)

For copyright permission requests, or for information about special discounts available for bulk purchases, sales promotions, or educational needs, write to or e-mail the publisher at one of the following addresses.

Phantasy Publishing LLC
35 Brooks Drive
Bethalto, IL 62010

Website: www.phantasypublishing.com
E-mail: support@phantasypublishing.com

This is a work of fiction. Names, characters, places, and incidents are either the products of the author's imagination, or they are used fictitiously. Any resemblance to actual persons, living or dead, businesses, companies, events, or locales is entirely coincidental.

Published in the United States of America

Table of Contents

CHAPTER 1

Late February 1880
St. Louis, Missouri

Mary Williams stood over the open grave with tears gently running down her face. She had lost so many of her family in the last year. First, her father died from a heart attack. Then, the cholera epidemic hit the city. She lost her little three-year-old son, Benji and then her husband of five years, Ben. She still felt empty not to be able to hold his little body on her shoulder as she carried him up to sleep each night. She and Ben had had such a happy marriage! It didn't seem fair to have it end so tragically. She packed up her possessions and moved in with her mother who had been ailing. That was six months ago. Now, here she was burying her last remaining family member. Her mother had caught pneumonia a few weeks ago. She had never been strong after her father died; she just sort of gave up trying to live. She fell asleep and never woke up. Mary didn't know what she was going to do.

She looked up from staring into the freshly dug grave and met the eyes of Lily Peters, one of her best friends. She saw the concern in her eyes and the empathy in her face. She would survive; she was a strong woman, she would do whatever she needed to live through this pain.

At five feet two inches, she looked like a strong wind would blow her away. Ben had always told her that God had packed a lot of woman in her tiny body. She didn't consider herself very pretty. Her long thick dark brown hair was wrapped into a bun on the top of her head and all that hair looked to snap her small neck with all the weight it held. She had amber colored eyes that always looked at the bright side of things. When Mary smiled, her eyes and whole face lit up and it looked like she was smiling with her entire body. She didn't realize that she was an extremely lovely young woman.

She tried to focus on the minister's words, but her mind kept wondering to what she was going to do now that she no longer had her mother to care for or a family to take care of. She was a very good seamstress and often made dresses for her friends. She thought of making clothes for the General Store or one of the dress shops that lined the streets. She was lucky that her mother's home was paid for and so was the little home that had been Ben and hers. They had a few acres, some chickens, a cow, a couple horses and a buggy. She had been going back every morning to milk the cow and gather the eggs. These she had used in baking for her mother and herself. She needed to make some decisions about what she was going to do and where. In the back of her mind was the possibility of moving somewhere else and starting over. There were too many painful memories here in St. Louis. But where would she go?

She was jarred out of her quiet thoughts when the minister asked her to take a hand full of dirt and throw it on her mother's casket. It just made her death all that much more final, but Mary did as he asked and then watched as the other mourners each did the same. Lily came and took Mary by the arm and led her away. She knew she was overcome with grief. So much had happened to poor Mary in the last year it didn't bear thinking about. She wanted to help her, but wasn't quite sure how yet. Together they climbed into the buggy her husband, Wes, had waiting.

The three rode back to Mary's mother's house in silence. It was Wes who broke into her thoughts.

"Mary, it doesn't bear thinking about all you've lost the past year. Maybe you need to move away and start over somewhere else. I know that I for one couldn't bear to see the house where Lily and I lived without her there. If you sell your house and your mother's, you would have enough money to travel to wherever you wanted to go and still have some left over to begin a different life for yourself. You're a damn fine seamstress and you could open up your own little store and make dresses for all the women from miles around. It would be enough to support you until you found someone else to love and settle down.

"It's not that I want you to go away, I know that both Lily and I would miss you something fierce. But we really want what would be best for you. It's too much to think about today, but in a day or two, give it a thought. You know if there was anything that Lily or I can do, you only have to ask and we will do it." Wes told her in a gentle voice. Mary felt lucky to have such good friends at this time in her life. Wes was a U.S. Marshall and even though he sometimes had to travel for his work, he and Lily were very happy.

She and Lily had gone to school together from first grade to when they graduated. They even went to St. Louis's Teacher College together for a year. Then they had each gotten married. It had been so much fun having them as friends. Lily had even been Benji's godmother when she had him baptized. She knew that her grief was theirs.

"I appreciate all you and Lily have done for me. I don't know what I would have done without you here beside me. I don't know what I'm going to do. I just need time to think. I promise to let you know as soon as I decide anything." Mary told them as she climbed out of the buggy. She waved good bye and walked into the dark, empty house to change out of her black dress. She needed to

3

go back to her own home and milk the cow and collect the eggs and feed the animals for the day. She was really glad to have something to do that would take her mind off things for a little while at least.

Her late husband hadn't been a very big man in size, but he was a good man, a gentle father and a loving husband. Mary changed into a pair of his pants and one of his shirts to ride the horse back to her own home. It only took her a few minutes and soon enough she was feeding the chickens, cow and horses; and gathering the eggs and milking the cow. It was while she was working that she was visited by one of her old neighbors, Tilly Wilson.

"How are you doing, Mary? I didn't think I'd see you today. I expected to find one of your friends' husbands doing this for you." Tilly began, "I was hoping to talk to you about selling this house and few acres of yours to my son and his wife. They're moving out from Springfield, Illinois to be closer to me in my old age. They don't want to be living with me, but have their own place. Your house and barn would fit them to a tea! Will you let me have first crack at owning the land if you decide to sell?"

"It would be a blessing to only have to worry about one house right now, Tilly. I'd like to see someone else living in it and enjoying it like Ben and I did. I'd love for you to buy it and anything else they want that we own. There's furniture inside the house, then there's the animals and buggy in the barn. I'd be willing to part with them too. I can't take them to my mother's house, and I know how much you enjoyed getting eggs and butter from me these last few years. Now your son and his wife will be able to continue the tradition." Mary told her with a tired smile. "I really don't know how much to even ask you to pay for the land and the house and barn. We probably need to ask one of the real estate brokers in town how much would be fair. I don't want them to pay too much, and I could sure use the money, so I don't want them to pay too little either. What if I talk to one of them and get back to you?"

"Oh, Mary, I'm so excited to have them living so close to me after all these years! Thank you so much! I'm going in and get my purse and go to the telegraph office and send them a wire right away!" Tilly gave Mary a little hug and almost ran to her own home two doors down from Mary's.

Well that solves one problem, Mary thought. Now what do I do with the other house? I will still need to go through the house and decide what I want to keep and take with me. I'll also need an inventory of all I'm leaving. I sure hope that the realtors know what to ask for the house, furniture and animals. It's been hard coming back with Ben and Benji gone. Mary finished milking and taking the milk and eggs with her, she went back to her mother's house.

She was up early the next morning to go talk to her friend, Brenda Smith. She worked in a realtor's office and she would know who to talk to if she didn't know herself about the selling of her home.

"Mary! What brings you out so early in the morning?" Brenda greeted her smiling.

"I need some help in selling Ben's and my house. Tilly has one of her son's moving to St. Louis and she wants to buy it, some of the furniture and the animals in the barn. It would be a pretty good set-up to move into. But I don't have a clue how much to ask for anything. Would you or someone you work for be able to help me out?" Mary asked her quietly.

"We sure do! Let me call George to go over and walk through it with you. You can let him know what pieces of furniture you want to keep and what you want to get rid of. He'll look over the barn and the critters you have and come up with a fair price. We'll help you with all the paper work and get you a good price, too. You just wait right here while I go talk with him." Brenda was gone and back within minutes. "I told George where your home was, and he said he'd meet you there in thirty minutes. Will that be alright?"

"It's perfect, Brenda! Thank you so much for getting his help. I'll be there waiting. I'm going to head over there now and look things over and decide what I want to take with me." Mary headed out the door and drove her buggy to her old house. She had a pad of paper so she could make her own notes of what she wanted to keep and get rid of. Tilly saw her drive up and came over to tell her what her son had told her.

"Mary! I'm so glad you're here, I was going to walk down to your mother's house in a little bit to talk to you! I'm just so excited that everything is working out so well! My son wired me back to tell me, the house and set-up sound perfect, they'll take anything you want to leave behind! And the best part is they'll be here in three days. They just have to pack up and take the train to St. Louis!" Tilly was so happy she was almost dancing!

"I'm so glad Tilly! George from the realtor's office is meeting me in thirty minutes to walk through the house and the barn to tell me how much everything is worth. It might be a good idea if you came with us to tell us if what I leave is something your son and daughter-in-law will want. How does that sound?" Mary asked her.

"Perfect! Let me just grab some paper and pen to write down all they'll have when they arrive. Also, I'll take over the milking and gathering of the eggs so you won't have to come out here every day. That way I'll have time to make them some butter before they even get here, and they'll have eggs and milk when they arrive." Tilly was off to get her own pad of paper.

Mary took the time to go into the house by herself. She steeled herself against all the emotions that hit her as she opened up the door. She wanted to have some things to remember Ben and Benji by when she gave up their house. Ben had been an inventor as well as a handy man. He had installed a grinder for meat on her counter. She'd take that with her. And the rollers she used to wash and rinse the clothes and wring them out so they would dry quicker, she wanted to take that with her, too. She picked up the nutcracker he had made and they had spent many winter nights cracking nuts and picking the sweetmeats out of them to eat and cook with. Then she saw the two rockers sitting in front of the fireplace. He had made them when she was expecting Benji. She would definitely take them with her. She would take all the quilts, feather mattresses, sheets and towels. She couldn't bring herself to part with them. She took one of their trunks from her bedroom and started putting in the items she wanted to keep.

Several hours later, she had everything she wanted packed in three trunks. Plus the rockers and her sewing machine, there was no way she'd leave it behind. George had come up with a fair price for the house, barn, animals and furniture. Tilly had agreed. They would all show up at his office tomorrow morning for the transfer of the funds from Tilly to Mary. He even offered to carry the three trunks, sewing machine and the rockers back to her mother's house today for her. Mary looked back on the little house that had held so much happiness and so much sorrow. She wanted to begin again. She didn't know how much more she could face until she broke down and cried over her loss all over again. She knew it was for the best, but it didn't make it any easier for her to make the decision. Maybe tomorrow would be a better day.

CHAPTER 2

Mary walked to the realtor's office the next morning. The sun was shining brightly on the last of the snow that still could be seen. Spring was Mary's favorite time of the year. She loved the smell of freshly dug dirt and being able to plant in her garden. There were always more vegetables than they could ever eat or can, and flowers were planted all over her yard and beside her porches. Ben had loved to go out into the woods and dig up more blooming plants for her every time he got the chance. Watering them and keeping them weeded were some of Mary's favorite things to do. Taking care of Ben and Benji had been her life and she had thrived in their love. She was a good daughter and had helped with the care of her father and then her mother without harboring any resentment. She wished she knew what she was going to do with her future.

Tilly was waiting at the realtor's office with a check for the house, barn, animals and furniture. She couldn't wait to sign the papers making her house her son's! Mary had to smile over her enthusiasm. She was glad that something good was coming out of all her sorrow. She knew how lonely Tilly had been and had often invited the older lady over to share a meal with her family. She had often looked after Benji while she worked with Ben on one of his handy-man jobs that required more than two hands to get it done. She had learned a lot from Ben on the use of tools and how to get things done. She was going to miss working with Ben almost as much as she would cooking for him and cleaning for both of her men.

After Tilly left, Brenda sat down with her to ask her about what she planned to do now that her mother was gone.

"I wish I knew, Brenda. Everything reminds me of Ben or Benji or my folks. It's hard to know that every day is going to be the same with the same loneliness I feel. Do you have any suggestions?" Mary asked her out of politeness rather than in hearing her ideas on the subject.

"Well, as a matter of fact I do. But before I tell you what I've got in mind, I want your promise that you'll hear me out till I've said the entire idea. Can you do that no matter how outrageous it sounds like?" Brenda asked her and guided her to sit down in one of the chairs before the fireplace in the office.

"Now I'm scared of what you're going to say!" Mary told her, "But I promise to sit here until you're done. The worst thing might be I'll just tell you 'no' and go home!"

"Alright, here goes nothing! You know that I have a sister who married a no-account gambler and moved out west. Well, Maggie has a house in the town of Pine City in Wyoming Territory. She runs a boarding house to make ends meet. She wrote me about three months back about a family that lived on a ranch just outside of town. Maggie and Cate were friends. Cate was married to a real nice rancher and they had five children.

"Well, about four months ago, Cate died leaving her husband and all those children. Her husband can't run his ranch and take care of all those kids. It seems that he tried to hire a housekeeper but nobody would dare take on five children for what he could pay. He got desperate enough to try to get a bride through one of those Mail-Order Bride places, but again nobody wants to take on a husband and five children. I've been thinking about you, Mary. You're so good with children, that five wouldn't be anything you couldn't handle. You're one of the best cooks I've ever seen and you've been running a household for over five years so there shouldn't be anything you haven't already done before.

"Think about it Mary. Those poor little motherless children need someone to spoil them and love them to make up for losing their mother. You need to be doing something that you feel matters. Taking care of five children and helping the rancher out would be something that would make a wonderful difference to that family." Brenda paused to let all her information sink in before she continued. "You'd be leaving all the sad memories behind and starting out someplace new. Maggie tells me that Cade, that's the husband's name, doesn't want another wife or any more children. But he realizes that the only way he can get someone to come out and help him raise those children, is to marry again. So, you'd both really be marrying again in name only. If at some time in the future, you and Cade feel differently about each other, then you can change the arrangement. What do you think about my idea or rather Maggie's and my idea?"

"I'm speechless, Brenda! Has Maggie approached Cade with this idea?" Mary asked her. "And if she has, what does he say? This is a lot to take in. I'll need time to think about it."

"It's a huge decision and I know you'll want to think about it before you do or make any rash commitments. I do have a letter from Cade. It's a copy of the one he sent to the Mail-Order Bride place. You read it and tell me what you think." Brenda handed her a letter written in bold letters:

Dear Madam,

I am writing this letter to ask you to come to the Wyoming Territory to my ranch. I am a widower with five motherless children. They are three, five, seven, nine and eleven. Four of them are boys and one is my daughter. I can't work the land or take care of my herd of cattle and still take care of the children. Five children is enough, I would be agreeable to a marriage in name only. If you think you are up to cooking, cleaning, washing and caring for my children, please wire me immediately. Looks don't matter; I just want a good woman taking care of my family.

Sincerely,
Cade Murphy

Mary read the letter over twice more before she handed the letter back to Brenda. "I feel for his plight; Brenda and the motherless children call out to me. But I'm just not sure. Let me think about it and I'll get back to you. I know he's in dire straits, so I'll try not to take too much time to decide. Thank you for thinking of me and writing your sister about me. I'll get back to you within the next few days."

"Thank you, Mary. I know you'll make the right decision. When you decide, we'll wire Maggie either way. You go home and think about it." Brenda told her and walked her to the door.

Mary immediately walked over to her friend Lily's house to tell her about the offer of marriage to a rancher in Wyoming. She needed a clear headed thinker to help her sort out all her fears and hopes of the situation. Lily was indeed home and welcomed Mary inside and to a cup of tea.

"Lily, I need your help in deciding an important decision. I know you'll tell me what you really think about the situation and you'll help me come to a good decision." Mary said to her and then told Lily all about the letter and Brenda's sister, Maggie in Wyoming and the poor motherless children and the rancher who was trying to do what's best for his family even though he doesn't want to get married again or have any more children. Lily listened to the entire story and then sat back in her chair and gave a huge sigh.

"Mary, I think you've already decided. You feel so much for the children and you've called them poor and motherless three times. Wes and I both think you should leave St. Louis and start over somewhere else. Wyoming sounds like the perfect place to me. You'd have a destination, you wouldn't be alone anymore, and you'd have children to fill your aching arms again. You'd make some lucky rancher a wonderful wife and mother to his children. Are you ready to make that jump?" Lily asked her wisely.

"I think I am. I would be helping someone out who really needs the help. I'd be surrounded by little ones. It would be in name only. I'm not ready to fall in love with someone else so soon after Ben and he's not ready to fall in love with anyone else after losing his wife of all those years and children. I think we can make it work as long as he's a reasonable man to work with. The call of those children is almost deciding for me. But what if he doesn't want me after all? Maybe somebody else has answered the letter by now." Mary was fearful yet oddly excited about traveling clear across the country and starting all over again without the memories everywhere she went.

"The only thing to do is to send a telegram to Maggie and find out if Cade still wants a wife and mother for his children. Then you can make your decision on how soon you can be packed and on your way!" Lily put on her coat and went with Mary back to see Brenda. She was happy for her friend, but, oh how she was going to miss having her in St. Louis!

Brenda immediately sent a wire to her sister and they all waited in the telegraph office for a reply. They didn't have to wait very long. Maggie's reply said:

'Cade is still looking for someone to fill the slot of a wife and mother. I'm riding out to see him today and find out if he wants to take a chance on your friend, Mary. I will send another telegram as soon as I know. Love, Maggie.'

Mary, Lily and Brenda walked out of the telegraph office in a state of expectation. She promised to let them know as soon as she heard anything. In the meantime, she was sending George back over to her mother's house to give her an estimate of what she could sell it for. She told Mary that they were going to be ready either way!

Mary spent the next few hours deciding what to keep and what to get rid of. She even made the decision to start packing what she was going to keep. How was she going to take all her possessions with her all the way to Wyoming?

She was constantly asking herself if she were doing the right thing.

Wyoming Territory, 1880

Maggie drove her horse and small buggy out to the Cade's ranch. She hoped he still wanted to find someone to help him out with his children. Mary Williams sounded like the perfect person to help him out and help raise those children. She missed her friend Cate and hoped if Mary came out to Wyoming that they might be friends. It would be nice to hear how Brenda was doing after all this time. They sent letters regularly back and forth, but it wasn't the same as seeing her sister again.

She arrived in time to see Cade chopping wood beside the house. It had been a while since she had been out to see the Murphy household. Cate had been sick for almost a year before she died. Unfortunately, the house and surrounding buildings looked in desperate need of some helping hands. She knew that Cade's oldest two children were big enough to help out, but she also knew that

Cade also needed them to help him with the herd of cattle and getting the land ready for planting.

"Hello, Maggie. It's good to see you. What brings you out this way?" Cade asked her and helped her out of the buggy. He hoped she was bringing him good news, he could sure need some. It had been a long year with Cate sick. He didn't know how much longer he was going to be able to hold on by himself.

"I hope I finally have some good news for you Cade. I think I've found you a wife!" Maggie told him. She watched his mouth drop open in surprise and hurried on with her explanation. "My sister lives in St. Louis and she has a friend who recently lost her husband and small son. Then her mother died leaving her all alone. Brenda, my sister, said she'd be the perfect person for you. She's wonderful with children, she has a teacher's certification, she's a great cook and usually a really happy person to be around. She's considering your letter to the Mail-Order Bride place, but she wants to know if you're still of a mind to getting a wife to help out around here. Are you?"

"Hell, yes I am! I didn't know when I would be able to start working in the fields and still take care of the little ones. We're about to starve from my cooking and you can see how run-down everything looks because I just don't have enough hours in the day to get everything done. What do I have to do to tell her to come and how soon can she be here?" Cade asked her without hesitation. He just might be getting that luck he needed desperately.

"I'm going to go back to town and wire my sister. She'll let me know when to expect Mary. Mary Williams is the women's name who is thinking about your letter asking about getting a Mail Order Bride. As soon as I hear back when to expect her, I'll let her know. I hope everything works out for you, Cade. Cate would be glad too. She wouldn't want you to lose the ranch after all you two put into it. She loved this ranch and you and all your children. I really think it's the only decision you can make at this time."

"Please wire your sister to get Mary on the next available train to Wyoming. The children and I will meet her in Cheyenne with a wagon to carry her and everything she wants to bring with her to Pine City. We'll get the nearest preacher to marry us and then I'll bring her home. She'll have her hands full, that's for sure, but I've got to start plowing in the next two weeks in order to get the entire crop planted. You know what a short growing time we have here. Just let me know when to expect her." Cade hesitated then grabbed Maggie's hand and shook it. "Thank you Maggie, you have been the answer to my prayers!"

Chapter 3

Maggie did indeed send a wire to St. Louis. It read:

> "Cade Murphy still wants a bride to take care of his children...Needed as soon as possible...Send time of arrival into Cheyenne...He will meet the train to carry all your things to his home...will wed in Pine City...Maggie."

Brenda rushed over to give the wire to Mary. Mary took a deep breath and said to go get George, she needed to sell her house and get a train ticket. Brenda squealed and hugged Mary at the good news. Then she ran back to the realtor's office to get George and get things rolling. It was going to be a very busy couple of days!

George and Brenda bought her mother's house and with the profits of the two sales, Mary had more than enough to buy her ticket to Wyoming and still have enough left over to help her get settled in Wyoming. She would leave in two days and travel by train for the next ten days to arrive in Cheyenne. A wire was sent to Maggie to take to Cade. Mary packed all her trunks, there were four in all and also filled two wooden boxes with items she wanted to take with her. She called Tilly in to take some of the remaining items over to her old house in the hopes that her son and his wife would be able to use them.

George carried all the trunks, boxes, sewing machine, both rockers and her two satchels to the train station and got them loaded. Lily and Brenda went with her to say good bye. They were really going to miss her, but they really felt like she needed to start over. And this was the perfect way to get her out and back into enjoying life again. After all, they could go visit her sometime very soon to see how she was doing.

Mary had sewed the money into the hem of her jacket. George had told her not to carry too much with her in her purse just in case it got stolen. He also gave her a small caliber gun to carry with her at all times. He didn't want anything bad to happen to Mary on her way out west. Brenda gave her a small basket with some sandwiches, some fruit and a pint of water to drink along the way. Lily and Wes gave her a book about Wyoming to read on the train. Mary was touched at the thoughtfulness of her friends. She would miss them so much! They all cried as the conductor called 'All aboard!' for the last time. Mary kissed them all good bye and climbed aboard for an adventure of a lifetime!

Ten days is a long time to spend on a moving train! Mary was dusty, gritty from lack of a good night's sleep and worried about what she would encounter when she arrived in Cheyenne. What if Mr. Murphy took one look at her and decided that she wouldn't do at all? What if she took one look at Mr. Murphy and she decided that he wouldn't do at all? Finally, she just decided to enjoy the ride and the beautiful scenery and let it all rest in God's hands.

Mary couldn't believe the difference in the landscape. Missouri had rolling hills and miles and miles of green grass. Kansas was as flat as a pancake and there was nothing but brown grass for as far as the eye could see. Colorado was beautiful with mountains and valleys of everything green. Wyoming wasn't as green, but she could still see mountains in the very distant countryside. She could see the ground waking up to spring in the amount of green she saw. Every day it grew more and more like the spring she was used to back home.

Seeing buffalo for the first time was humbling. These magnificent animals looked majestic on the range, she couldn't get over how many there were! It seemed like there were thousands in every herd they encountered. They covered the ground as far as the eye could see. She found it hard to believe that they had been reduced to a small reduction of what their numbers used to be.

As Mary pulled into the Cheyenne train depot, she washed her face with her handkerchief and some of the water she refilled at every stop to drink. She combed her hair into a bun at the back of her head, tried to shake out the wrinkles and dust of her dress, buttoned up her jacket and grabbed her basket of food and her purse. She took a deep breath and climbed off the train. She looked around for her trunks and other belongings and breathed a sigh of relief when she found it all safely stacked along the walkway. Then she started looking for Cade Murphy. Not knowing what he looked like, she decided to look for a man with a lot of children. She didn't think that too many families had five children in them!

It took her a few minutes to find them. They were sitting in a wagon being pulled by two mules. They looked like stair steps when they stood up to jump down from the wagon or for the little ones to be lifted carefully down and put on the ground. Then she took a good long look at their father. He was big, very big, Mary decided. Ben hadn't been much taller than she was. Cade's oldest boy looked to be about as tall as she was! She was about to marry into a family of giants, Mary thought! In his favor, he was a good looking man in a mountain man kind of way. His hair was too long and he needed a shave. His clothes were dusty from traveling by wagon so far. And he looked as nervous as she was. She smiled and waved to let him know that she was the one he was looking for. When he realized that she was waving at him, he looked once and then looked again. My God! Were all those trunks and boxes hers? What could she possibly be bringing with her? And then he took another look at Mary. She was tiny, hardly bigger than his children! How could she possibly be expected to do all that was required to take care of the house and children? What had he gotten himself in for now?

Mary saw the look of shock and surprise come over his face. She knew without him saying a word that he was disappointed in her. She took a deep breath and reached out her hand, "I take it that you're Cade Murphy?" At his short nod, she continued. "Well, I am Mary Williams, you're intended. I hope that we will have a very good relationship and I look forward to meeting all your children."

Cade shook her hand, surprised at how strong her grip was. Maybe she was hardier than she looked. He gave her a second and then a third look. She was prettier than he thought she might be, not that looks were all that important he reasoned. But at least she wouldn't curdle the milk with her looks; he smiled a little for having made a joke. "Hello, Mary. Welcome to Wyoming!"

"Is this all your stuff?" At her nod, he told her to step aside; he and his boys would load it all up in nothing flat. As they grabbed her trunks and boxes, she was amazed at how strong they all were. Picking up her heavy trunks seemed like child's play to them. All except the one that held all her books. That one, Cade gave her a sideways glance and then picked it up with a grunt. They put her boxes in the wagon and then the large roll of feather mattresses. He picked up the sewing machine and each of his sons picked up one of the rockers. In minutes they had her loaded up and started putting the children back into the wagon. As he lifted up the smaller three, he told her their names.

"This is Cooper, he's three. This is Cody, he's five. Here's my only daughter, Kit who's seven. The older two boys are Cameron and Christian, they're nine and eleven. I'm thirty-two by the way and you are...?" Cade asked as he lifted her up into the wagon.

"I'm twenty-three, Mr. Murphy. And I am really glad to meet you all today. I hope we get along really well after we get to know one another. How long is it to your ranch...Cade?" Mary asked.

"It's a five-hour trip. We left at four this morning to get here in time to meet the train at nine o'clock. We should reach Pine City to get married about two this afternoon. It'll be another hour after that before we reach the ranch. Get comfortable. It's a long way to travel." He told her as he backed up the wagon and started out of town.

Five hours in this wagon after being on the train for the last ten days, Mary was aghast at the vast distances these people traveled and thought nothing of it. As the wagon lumbered along, Mary dreamed of a hot bath at the end of her journey and a hot meal.

CHAPTER 4

There was silence as they traveled on the bumpy road. Mary smiled at the quiet children. She wasn't used to little children being so silent. Mary tried to start a conversation with her intended new husband.

"Cade, tell me about your ranch and what to expect. I've never been very far from St. Louis before and this trip has been an experience I'll never forget. I couldn't get over the difference in the landscape from state to state or to territory. Missouri is mostly green at this time of year. We have hills, but no mountains. Kansas was so flat and it wasn't that green at all." Mary told all of the Murphy family as they bumped along. "I really liked Colorado with its mountains, rivers and valleys. I didn't know what to expect from Wyoming. My friends gave me a book on the Wyoming Territory. But there were no pictures showing how beautiful it is. It looks a lot like the Colorado Territory. I can even make out the mountains in the far distance. They look almost purple against the skyline...I understand that you have really severe winters with snow several feet thick! I can't imagine that much snow at any one time.

"We have snow in St. Louis and sometimes it reaches the height of almost a foot high, but that's an accumulation of snow from several different times that the snow fell. Are you used to winters like that?"

Cade swallowed a few times and nodded his head. He didn't know what to think about the tiny little woman sitting next to him. Her voice was low and soothing as she talked, he found he liked listening to her. He wasn't used to talking much himself. He was a quiet man and his children had taken his lead. They didn't talk much either. He noticed her looking at him in expectation. She was probably waiting for him to talk in answer to her many questions.

"Yes, ma'am, we do get lots of snow up here. We have a short growing season from late April to the beginning of August. We've been known to get snow as soon as late August and get it as late as early May. It's not unusual to have a foot or more each time it snows. We've learned to be ready with plenty of food stored in the case of blizzards or Nor'easters. When they come, it's not safe for man nor beast out in the cold." Cade offered in reply.

"What do you do to keep your cattle safe during these times? I know your barn can't be that big to house all those animals!"

"They're pretty rugged animals. I don't like longhorns, like some of the ranches around me have. They're too unpredictable and too many cowboys end up getting hurt just trying to handle them. We've got white faced Herefords. They're big and in winter they get real heavy coats of hair covering them. Even so, they manage to find some sheltering valley or stand of trees. We don't usually lose too many to the cold. We try to take food out in the wagon when it gets really deep because they won't be able to find any food on the ground." Cade told her with some assurance.

"I suppose you'd like to hear a little about me." Mary told him. She found a space ahead of the mules and stared at it as she told him about her late husband and little boy. "We were married for five years. They were good years. My husband was a handy-man and an inventor. He tried to make us as comfortable as he could. Benji was our little boy; he was three when he died. Ben and Benji both died from a cholera epidemic that swept through St. Louis last fall. I tried to take care of my elderly mother, but she died from pneumonia a few weeks ago...I needed to start over someplace where there weren't too many memories." Mary's voice kind of dwindled away as she told him about Ben and Benji. There was silence for a while and then Cade told her about Cate.

"Cate and I were sweethearts from the time we were in grade school. We just knew that we would get married someday. The only time we were apart was for the two months that I came ahead and filed on land and then I went back to get Cate. Cate was sixteen and I was eighteen when we got married and came out west to Wyoming for the Homestead Act. We could file on one hundred-sixty acres for free if we built a house on it and stayed in it for five years. We lived in a tent for the first year. We built a sod house the next summer. We lived in the sod house for almost ten years. Course, we built on a couple more rooms as we needed them for the children. Any time we got any money ahead, we bought more land and more cattle.

"It took us almost ten years to finally build a cabin of logs. But by then we had over a thousand acres and almost three hundred head of cattle. We never borrowed from the bank, so everything we have is paid for lock, stock and barrel. It's not the fanciest place out here, but we make do. Cate started feeling puny after Cooper was born. It started out by just feeling tired all the time and not having very much energy. By the time Cooper was two, she was in bed for most of every day. She tried her best to keep us fed and clothed, but she just wasted away before our very eyes.

"The older boys and Kit tried to keep an eye on the little ones, but they always had their own chores to do. It takes all of us to keep a roof on the cabin and food on the table. I tried to do it all when Cate died, but I'm certainly no cook that's for certain! Cleaning isn't my bag either. I'm afraid that you'll find the cabin a little on the dirty side. We don't have much for supplies either, but I figure once you get settled that you'll want to go get your own supplies to cook and what not. We keep a tab at the General Store,

Jonah Clark the owner and mayor of Pine City will let you put whatever you feel we need on my tab. I'll pay it back when I sell my crops in the fall." Cade paused; surprised that he talked so much. Mary sure was easy to talk to!

"I'll take over as much of your load as I can, Cade. I'm used to cooking, cleaning, washing clothes, sewing, taking care of a garden and even helping milk the cow and gather eggs. Sometimes when my husband had a job that required more than his own two hands, I helped him out. I'm pretty handy with a hammer, nails and a saw! It won't be a perfect job, but I can get it done. I want to be a big help to you and your family." Mary told him and touched him on one of his enormous arms. Cade felt the warmth of her touch long after she had removed her hand.

"I don't know how much work a little thing like you can do!" Cade told her bluntly.

Mary laughed at his statement. "You'd be surprised how much I can get done, Mr. Murphy! I may be little but I'm strong, organized and don't tire easily! I won't make any promises, but I think you'll be pleasantly surprised how nice I'll make your cabin for you and your children."

"I'd like that, Mary. I won't be much help for the next couple of months. I've got to start plowing tomorrow or we won't have time for the crops to grow. We need the money from the harvest to pay off our debts at the General Store and buy land or cattle. I try to improve on our ranch every year. I won't need the boys, Cameron and Christian, for about a month while I'm plowing, harrowing and planting the fields. We'll have thirty acres in each of wheat, corn and oats. The boys chop wood for two hours every day. We've got to have eight to ten cords of wood to get us through the winter plus we still need wood in the spring, summer, and fall for cooking and keeping the cabin warm. That's a lot of logs to cut down and chop up. But as soon as they get done, they'll lend a hand for you."

24

"I'd like that! I'm sure that all the children will help us fix up the cabin and put in a garden. We won't let you down, Cade." Mary told him looking into his dark blue eyes. Cade heard her but he didn't quite believe her. He worried he was making a terrible mistake making her his wife, but he just didn't have a choice! He needed to start plowing tomorrow if he was going to get everything in the ground in time to grow. He felt like he just had to take a chance on this young lady. He hoped God was finally smiling down on him and had sent him a worthy helpmate for his family.

"Are you goin' to be our new Ma?" A little voice asked from behind Mary on the wagon.

"If it's alright with your father, I'd like to be your new Ma very much, Cooper." Mary smiled at the youngest Murphy encouraging him to talk some more, but he just smiled and went back to looking out the side of the wagon.

"No offense, Ma'am, the little kids need a Ma, but Cameron and me do just fine on our own." Christian told her bluntly.

"How much schooling have you had, Christian?" Mary asked him with a smile.

"I ain't ever been to school. Too far to go and I don't see any need for book learning. I'll get along just fine the way I am." Christian retorted.

"I agree it's too far to go to school, but I've been trained to be a teacher. I was hoping to be able to teach you all at home in the evenings, especially during the winter when we'll have more time each day to spend on it." Mary let that sink in before she added, "Working and running a ranch are admirable ambitions, but what if you wanted to be something other than a rancher? Have you ever thought of becoming a doctor, a lawyer, or even a veterinarian?"

"What's that?" Cameron said with some hesitation.

"A veterinarian is an animal doctor. With all the cattle you have on your ranch, an animal doctor sounds like he could be pretty handy to have around." Mary went on to tell them. "Just think about it, I would never try to force you to learn to read and write. That choice has to be up to you."

By now they were coming into Pine City and Cade drove the tired mules to one of the side streets beside a white church with a tall steeple. He helped Mary down and then each of his five children. Together they walked into the church to the waiting minister. They were married less than ten minutes later and Mary held a marriage certificate in her hands. It had all happened so fast her head was still spinning. But nevertheless, they were married in sickness or in health till death does them part! They both were thinking of their late wife and husband. They knew they would understand the haste in which they were joined, but it didn't make them feel any better about the ceremony.

Without stopping for supplies, they continued to drive the tired mules out to the ranch. Mary paid particular attention how to get back to town for the supplies he was sure she would need. The road they traveled was well used and didn't seem as rough or bumpy as the previous road. Maybe she was just too tired to notice. They were pulling into a lane on the left before too long and Mary got her first glance of her new home.

It was a huge disappointment to what she expected. The cabin was just that, a rectangular shaped building with no porch only a step to get into the front door. Logs lay everywhere, some half chopped; some still had limbs on them. The wood that was already chopped was lying exactly where it lay when it was chopped off the tree. The windows which were glass, Mary was glad to see, were too dirty to see into or out of. The barn sat behind the house by a pretty good distance. A corral could be seen to be leaning toward the ground. It looked like a strong wind would collapse the entire enclosure. She saw no chickens, cows, pigs, dogs, cats, or anything closely resembling any other animals except a huge ox eating grass in the tilting corral. Mary closed her eyes in the hope of when she opened them it would have been a mistake, but even when she opened up her eyes again. It sadly looked the same if not worse, because now they were even closer to the buildings.

Cade lifted her down and told her to go on into the house. He and the boys would unload the wagon and see to the care of the wagon and the mules. Maybe she could look around the kitchen and see what she could make for supper. They were all tired and hungry. Mary stepped up into the cabin. It was even worse inside than it had been outside!

There was just a huge L-shaped room with a fireplace along one side of the room and a cook stove on the other end. A table with seven mismatched chairs stood in the middle of the room. The table itself was covered with dirty dishes and food scraps. The stove hadn't been cleaned in a very long time. But the worst of it was that there was only a dirt floor! She would be living in a home with a dirt floor! How in heaven was she supposed to clean a dirt floor? Mary closed her eyes for a minute just to get enough energy to start making sense out of the mess she found herself in. What in all that was holy had she done in marrying Cade Murphy and coming out to this crude cabin? How was she going to extricate herself from her predicament? Jesus, Mary and Joseph, she was going to need all their help in making this cabin into a livable home!

CHAPTER 5

Before she could start on cleaning, Mary had to use the outhouse. She had been on the train and then over five hours traveling by wagon. Her bladder was not the size of a bucket and she was about to burst.

"Kit, where is the outhouse?" Mary asked the little girl.

"I'll show you. It's out the back door and back a piece." Kit told her in a whisper.

Mary followed and knew before she even stepped inside to use it that it was in as sad a shape as the rest of the house. But she was forced to use it no matter how bad it smelled! She made a mental note to get some lime and mesh to put over the holes she was going to cut into the door and the back wall. She would get some fresh air into the foul smell she found herself in.

She went back to the house to see what they had to cook with. To her dismay, there wasn't much to work with. She found some flour and a bucket of lard. No eggs. No milk. No butter. She finally found a side of bacon and started cutting off strips to cook up. She used the flour and lard to fashion a sort of biscuit and adding more wood to the cook stove, she put them in the oven. She cleaned out a skillet and started frying the bacon. She found some potatoes and cut them up to go with the bacon and the biscuits. She would definitely be going into town tomorrow to get some much needed supplies! The list kept growing longer and longer in her mind of what she would need to get at the General Store.

While the biscuits, potatoes and bacon were frying, she loaded up a pan with hot water from the reservoir on the stove and started washing off the table and the dishes that had been left on it. She noticed that her trunks, boxes, mattresses, sewing machine, rockers and valises were stacked to the right of the front door. While she washed the dishes, she had time to look around the cabin a little more. There was a room, a bedroom she supposed, in the square of the L-shaped room. She also noticed stairs, not a ladder, going up to the loft that ran the entire length of the cabin. I guess that's where the children sleep, Mary thought. She didn't see any beds, so she assumed that the children slept on pallets on the floor.

She had just dried the last of the dishes and set the table when the boys and Cade came in from the barn. All of them sniffed the air as they came in the back door. Something sure smelled good. They hadn't eaten since early this morning and that was just lumpy mush. Cade sure hoped she had cooked enough to feed them all. It took a lot of food to keep his family fed.

Mary brought the food to the table and motioned for everyone to sit down. They didn't have to be told twice! They all sat and started reaching for food. Biscuits were tossed to each other rather than passing the platter around. The biscuits were split and bacon was put between the top and bottom making a bacon sandwich for lack of a better name. Potatoes were scooped up and eaten faster than Mary had ever thought possible. What she had thought was a lot of food, disappeared quickly and they looked around hopefully for more!

"Well, I'm sorry there's no more, but I ran out of potatoes. I have just enough flour to make biscuits for breakfast in the morning. I will definitely start cooking a lot more food in the future! I will also have to go into town tomorrow to get some supplies. Will that be alright with you Cade?" Mary asked him eating the last biscuit and the only one she had been able to get.

"What you do each day, is up to you. I'll leave at first light to start plowing and you won't see me until it gets dark. After the boys have chopped wood for a couple of hours, they'll hitch up the mules and take you to town. You should be able to get what you need. If I should see a deer while I'm plowing, I'll try to shoot it, so you can have some fresh meat to work with."

"That sounds good. If you will all give me your dirty clothes, I'll wash them in the morning and have them ready for you to wear them the next day..." She noticed that they all looked dumbfounded at her news. "What's wrong? What did I say?"

"Mary, all the clothes we have are on our back. I just washed them three days ago, so they should still be good for a couple more days. Maybe with that fancy sewing machine you got, you can make us all a few shirts to wear." Cade told her. "Now, we've been up since before the sun this morning in order to get you from the train. Everybody head for the loft and get to bed."

They all jumped from the table and headed for the stairs. Cade told Mary good night and headed for the room in the corner. Mary was in shock. They didn't have any other clothes to wear! She started cleaning up the dishes as she thought and thought about all she would need tomorrow when she went to town. Exhausted, she finally laid down on the table with one of her quilts. Surely the morning would look better after a good night's sleep. Mary certainly hoped it would!

Mary was up at first light making the last of the flour and lard into biscuits. She fried up the last of the bacon and put on a pan of mush to go with it. It might not taste very good, but at least there would be enough to go around.

Cade came out of the bedroom while she was taking things off the stove, he sat down quietly. "Where did you sleep last night, Mary?"

"On the table wrapped in a quilt..." Mary told him and sat down beside him.

"We're married. I thought you'd join me in the bedroom. I wasn't going to demand any husbandly rights or anything, but I did think I would enjoy sleeping beside you in that bed each night." Cade told her as he ate his breakfast.

"You didn't say anything last night, and I didn't want to go where I wasn't wanted. I thought we'd have some time to sort things out this morning." She swallowed heavily and continued. "I will be glad to sleep with you instead of on the table."

That sounded funny to both of them and they smiled at each other more at ease with each other than they had the previous day.

"How did you get the mush so smooth? I tried everything I could think of and mine was always lumpy and runny. It tasted even worse than it looked!" Cade surprised her by saying.

"You just add a few grains of corn meal at a time." Mary responded. "Cade, I have money from the sale of my house and my mother's. Would you mind if I bought a few things that aren't necessities but would make things easier around here and maybe make it a little better?"

"What you do with your money is your business. I'll feed and take care of our family." Cade told her firmly.

"That will be fine. I'll charge the food we need at the General Store, but I'll use my money to get what I want from any other store you have in town. I promise not to spend it foolishly!" Mary told him. "I've made you up a little lunch to take with you when you go out into the fields. It's a long time till supper."

Cade was surprised at her thoughtfulness. "I appreciate it. You going to be alright with just the children around?"

"We'll be just fine. I think you'll be surprised at how much we get done while you're plowing the fields!" Mary told him, her thoughts listing all she wanted to get done to the cabin so it would be much more palatable to live in.

With a nod, Cade picked up his lunch and headed to the barn to hitch up the ox to the plow. He trusted that she couldn't get into too much trouble in one day. He was curious to see what she felt were 'necessities'!

Mary filled a large kettle with water from the reservoir. She washed out her clothes from the last few days on the train. It felt good to wash all over and to put on a clean dress. She combed her hair into one long braid down her back. She looked into the bedroom. She couldn't believe what she saw. The bed, Cade talked about was only about a foot off the floor. Even from the door, she saw that it sagged in the middle and almost touched the floor. Making a new bed for Cade and herself was also put on her growing list of things needed to be done.

She stripped the sheets and blankets off his bed and took them to the kitchen and started washing them in the kettle she had used to wash in. When everything was clean, she walked out the back door to hang the clothes but found there were no clothes lines to hand them on. She took them back into the kitchen and put them on the table. She rummaged in one of her trunks and found some rope. Heading back outside, she tied it to one of the lower limbs of the tree near the outhouse. She walked back to the house and nailed a nail into the side of the house and hooked the rope on the nail, and then she walked back to the tree to retie the rope. She now had two clothes lines to hang the sheets, blanket and her clothes on.

By then, Christian and Cameron came down from the loft. They ate huge amounts of biscuits, bacon and mush. They told her they would be chopping wood for a while and would let her know when they could go into town. She followed them outside.

"I'm not going to tell you what to do or anything, but what if you put two logs side by side and nailed them together. Then put a board on either end of the logs. That way you could stack the chopped wood and you'd have a lot more room to chop wood. It's just a suggestion." Mary smiled and returned to the house to start washing dishes.

Christian looked at Cameron and frowned. "She's not even here one day and already she's telling us how to do things!"

"Yeah, but you know it makes sense. You and I are always complaining that we're falling over each other and the wood that we chop. If we follow her suggestion, it would make a lot of room and make it easier to get wood for the stove and fireplace." Cameron told him. He looked up hopefully, "I say we do it, not because it was her idea, but it makes sense. Pa will be glad to get the mess cleaned up too."

"All right, we'll do it, not because she suggested it, but because it's a good idea and solves a problem for us." Both boys agreed and within fifteen minutes they had a couple of bars of wood to stack the wood on. Christian continued to chop wood and Cameron stacked the wood on the logs.

Both boys were very aware of what Mary was doing. They noticed the clothes lines where there had been none before. They also had to admit that her mush was a heck of a lot better than their father's had been. Mary came out of the house then and headed to the barn. She came out minutes later with a scythe. Walking to the front of the house, she started cutting down all the long grass that covered the front of the house and yard. It was very tall; it came past Mary's knees. Mary was worried that snakes could hide in the tall grass. When she finished the front, she cut the back of the house and under the clothes lines. She cut the entire area from the house to the barn. Then she came out with a rake and started raking up the loose grass. She proceeded to put the loose grass into pillowcases. Between the front yard and the back, she was able to fill seven pillowcases with grass. These she took into the house. They could hear her sewing machine running even chopping and stacking wood. What was she doing in there?

The sewing woke up the three little ones. Mary stopped sewing and washed their faces and hands and sat them down to breakfast. There wasn't much left but mush and a few biscuits. They didn't complain and ate every drop of food she had left. She asked the three of them if they would fill her wood box by the stove and the fireplace. She went up stairs and grabbed their pallets and blankets. She took them and washed them in the kettle she kept heated from the reservoir. She put them on the clothes lines with Cade's bedding. Then she took the hot water and went up into the loft and scrubbed the entire floor.

Still waiting on Christian and Cameron, she took what was left of her scrubbing bucket and took off for the outhouse. It looked worse in the day than it had last night. She scrubbed the seat, the walls, and she would have scrubbed the floor, but it had a dirt floor. Something else to add to her list of things to do! It's never ending, Mary thought. Then she went back inside the house and took out some paper and pencil from her satchels. She sat down at the clean kitchen table and started making her list of what she wanted to buy at the General Store and at other stores in town. It was rather long by the time she was done. Cameron and Christian finished chopping for the day and Mary had warm water for them to wash up in before they headed for town. While they hitched up the mules to the wagon, Mary took the money out of her jacket and put it in her drawstring purse. She was ready to go spend some money, both Cade's and hers!

CHAPTER 6

It was a beautiful spring day, but there was still a bite in the air. Christian and Mary sat on the seat with the other four children huddled behind them in the wagon. Mary was wondering how to bring up the subject of change. She felt they might be a little resistant to it from being their mother's house and all. But there were certain things that she felt would benefit the whole family. She finally took the bit between her teeth and started talking to Christian and made sure that Cameron was included in the conversation.

"Boys, the stacked wood sure looks nice..." Mary began. "I'd like to make some changes around the house in the next few weeks, but I'm going to need both of you to help me. We'll have plenty of work for the three little ones, too, but I simply don't have the muscle that the two of you do. I've tried chopping wood. It took forever to get enough wood just for the cook stove. I've got the energy, but not the muscle. Would you be willing to help me?"

Christian looked over his shoulder at Cameron, "Doing what exactly?"

"Well, I'd like to put in a wooden floor. I noticed where the water comes through the roof when it rains, so I'd like to put some roofing paper down and shingles on top of that for the house and the barn. The cabin needs to be chinked to keep the wind from blowing through; it'll make it warmer in the winter months with a wood floor, a solid roof and chinking between the logs. We'd do the same thing to the barn with the roof and chinking, but not a wooden floor.

"I'll need your help in making a better bed for your father and then five beds in the loft for each one of you. I'd like to separate the loft into three separate little rooms so you'll have some privacy as you dress. I want to get you all some more clothes and make some very warm coats for all of us for the winter. I plan on putting in a huge garden. We'll eat the fresh vegetables and I'll can enough for us to get through the winter with. I want popcorn, corn, green beans, beets, carrots, tomatoes, potatoes, sweet potatoes and onions.

"I want us to dig a cellar that is deep enough for your father to stand up in just in case we have a tornado, Indian attack, or have a reason to hide. I want to put a trap door in the kitchen that will lead to the cellar, so that we won't have to go outside to get supplies. I want to build a counter in the kitchen to house all the dishes, pots and pans and other cooking supplies that we have. I want to put in a large half barrel in the corner and put up blankets for privacy. We'll be able to take baths and we'll hook up rubber hoses to drain it just by pulling a plug. The water will go into our garden to help water it. We'll put another drain in the kitchen sink so we won't have to throw water out of it either. I want to put on a front porch and a shorter back porch. I want to get some chickens, some little piglets and a milch cow. We'll have to make some pens for the pigs, a coup for the chickens and the cow we'll just stake out.

"I want to build a smoke house so that when you see game, you shoot it and we have somewhere to put it so it won't go bad. I think we should build a corn crib to store the corn for the winter and possibly a silage shed for the stalks. The cattle could eat both if the winter is harsh. I intend to put up more clothes lines and a wash stand in the back yard that I can wash clothes from and also seal the jars I'll be canning. That should get us through the first few months. After that, I think we need a pump in the kitchen and in the barn, so that we can pump water even with three feet of snow outside. We'll probably need your father for that." Mary stopped to get a breath and saw the amazement on both boys faces. "Will you help me?"

"Lady, are you crazy?!!" Christian started, "We don't have that kind of money! Pa will go bonkers if you borrow money we don't have! Cameron and I won't help you make Pa mad, that's for sure!"

"One, I'm not going to borrow any money. Two, I have my own money that I'm willing to spend if it will help us get all of the work done and we end up in much better shape than we are now. Three, a couple loads of lumber, a couple rolls of chicken wire, several kegs of nails, some rolls of roofing paper and some pitching tar should just about do it for the extra supplies. Of course, I also plan on buying a dozen and a half chickens and a rooster, three piglets and a cow. The food supplies, I'll put on your father's account at the General Store. Now how do you feel?" Mary hoped she had convinced them they could indeed do all she had said.

"We don't know how to make pens or coups or even put in a wooden floor. We sure as hell don't know how to dig out a cellar or a smoke house. And then there's the roof, Cameron and I don't know how to put on shingles much less make them!" Christian frowned again, "I know you want to do the right thing, but I think you've bitten off more than you can chew!"

"What if I told you that I know how to do all those things? My husband was a handy-man and an inventor. Whenever he had a job that required more than two hands, I would help him. I know how to put on a roof, and I can show you and Cam how to make shingles. I know how to make a chicken coup, pig pen, kitchen counters and beds, lay a floor and build a cellar and a smoke house.

37

But I do need bigger muscles than I have. With all of us working together, I know that it's possible." Mary waited for the two boys to agree to her plan. It was Cameron who was the first to speak.

"I sure do like the idea of having a bed to sleep in instead of the loft on a pallet. The floor is hard and I would love not to have the wind slip through the logs. I say we help and see if we can indeed do all she says. It sure would make the cabin snug and warm, as well as the barn." He looked to Christian to see if he were going to agree too.

"Alright, we'll loan you our muscles and our strong backs. But if this doesn't work, don't blame us. Agreed?" Christian asked.

"Agreed!" Mary was thrilled to get there assistance. "Now one more thing..." She hesitated with a smile, "Would you boys mind if I shortened your names to Chris and Cam? It's a lot easier to say and I know we'll be talking an awful lot over the next month at least!"

Both boys smiled trying the shortened use of their names.

"Cam is fine with me, I kind of like it!" He smiled at her for the first time.

"Chris is fine with me, too. I've never liked my name; I felt it was a sissy name! Chris is good; I can live with it being shortened!" And then he too smiled at Mary for the first time. It was good beginning.

They were in town before you knew it. The blacksmith's and lumber yard were on the outskirts of town and Mary suggested that they stop there first. She bought hinges, hooks and a pulley from the blacksmith. She ordered 200 planks of 1" x 12" x 12' boards, 150 2" x 4"x 12' boards, 50 1" x 2" x 12' boards, a dozen 4" x 4" x 12' foot timbers, and six 2" x 2" x 12' boards. She paid the lumber yard in cash and asked them to deliver them to Cade Murphy's ranch today. They promised to have them delivered by noon at the latest.

Then they headed toward the General Store, but Mary saw the cooper smith's and asked them to stop to order some barrels.

Here she asked for a small keg to be cut length-wise, a small barrel to have three inches off and they wanted both ends, a huge half barrel for bathing and a half dozen buckets. He promised to get them over to the lumber yard and they would be delivered to them when they brought out the lumber. Her last stop before they got to the General Store was the wheelwright. Here Mary picked out three 24" inch wheels that they put in the wagon with the hinges.

"Now to the General Store!" Mary told the surprised children. If they were amazed at the amount she already had ordered, wait until they saw all she was ordering from here, Mary thought.

She looked with interest and noticed that they had two banks in Pine City, the First National Bank of Pine City and Pine City Bank. There were several saloons, a land office, several restaurants, a hotel, a shoe repair shop, a milliner's dress shop and a resale shop. Mary wondered if they sold used clothing. She sure hoped they did. Chris pulled up in front of the General Store and everyone piled out of the wagon. Mary pulled her list out of her purse and they marched in.

The first person she saw was about six feet tall. He had a pleasant face and a balding head. He wore a white apron over his slacks and white shirt. Mary smiled and introduced herself to him.

"I'm Mary...Murphy. I married Cade Murphy yesterday and we need a whole lot of supplies. He said you would put it on his tab." Mary began.

"Welcome to Pine City, Mrs. Murphy. I know Cade very well and know he hasn't bought any supplies since last summer. So I'm very sure there was hardly anything to cook with there. You tell me what you want and I'll get it loaded in your wagon, how's that? I'm Jonah Clark, by the way and that lovely lady over there is my wife

39

Olivia, but we call her Liv! Now let's write down what all you need." Jonah told her with a smile.

"I'll be giving you two lists, Mr. Clark. The food Cade will pay for, but I have some other items that I'll be paying for with cash if that's all right." Mary told him while looking around at the clean and stuffed store. She knew she could go crazy in this store and she needed to spend her money wisely in order to get everything they needed.

"That should be no problem. First tell me what to put on Cade's tab and then we'll deal with yours." Jonah told her grabbing a tablet of paper to write down everything she wanted.

Here goes Mary thought!

"I need 200# of flour and I want it either in a wooden barrel or a metal tin, so that it will keep a long time, 150# of sugar in tins, 50# of brown sugar, a bag of salt and one of pepper, 100#of rice and 100# of corn meal and another 100# of oatmeal. I want 150# of potatoes, 100# of carrots, 100# of onions, 2 5-gallon buckets of lard, a 100# bag of beans, kerosene in a five-gallon container. I need two large hams, three sides of bacon, a tin of baking soda, baking powder, a box of yeast, a barrel of vinegar, a bushel of dried apples, 24 cans of green beans, 24 cans of peaches, 30 cans of tomatoes, 2 bottles of vanilla, a small container of oregano, sweet basil, cinnamon, cloves, garlic and rosemary. I'll also need seeds to plant our garden. I'll need popcorn, corn, green beans, carrots, beets, tomatoes, onions, potatoes, sweet potatoes, cucumbers, green peppers and the seeds to grow oregano, basil, thyme and marjoram.

Mary hesitated before she continued, "Then on my list that I will pay for I want two rolls of chicken wire, a fine mesh roll, four kegs of nails—two of roofing and two of just nails, a butter churn, enough rubber tubing to stretch for 100 yards, corks, a sheet of tin about 30 inches by 24 inches, two rolls of roofing paper and a five-gallon bucket of tar. I'm going to walk around your store and pick up a few more items. We'll put them on the counter so you can add them to our list." Mary looked up and watched Jonah writing as quickly as she spoke.

"Ma'am, you can look all you want! This is some dandy of a list, or rather two lists. I'll have everyone in the store help get it ready!" Jonah smiled, he really liked the little lady. She knew what she wanted and didn't waste any time!

Mary looked up and down the crowded aisles of goods. She stopped at the axes and hatchets. She picked up two small hatchets and felt them for the weight of them, and then she reached up for two belts that the hatchets would ride in. "Chris, Cam put these around your waist and see if they feel alright."

When they did she said, "Take them up front to add to my bill." The surprised boys didn't need to be told twice. Then she headed to the shovels. She found two small shovels and gave them to Cody and Cooper to take up front, the shovels were for the boys. She picked up two brooms, one smaller than the other. She gave these to Kit and told her one was for her and the other one was for Mary. As she came to the counter, she told Jonah to add on 200# of chicken feed to the order.

"I'm in need of a dozen and a half chickens, three small piglets that we can fatten up for fall, and a milch cow. Can I purchase them from you or do you know where I can buy them?" Mary asked.

"I know where you can get them, and I'll add them to the bill and send them out to the ranch sometime today. Will that be all right?" He asked.

"Perfectly, by the way add on some lye soap. I'll only need a few bars of soap; I'll be making my own. I've thought of a few more items, Mr. Clark. Could you cut me a 10# roast of either venison or beef, a large package of fat from the cutting up of meat that I can make into tallow for the soap, and twenty-five candles. I noticed that you had a large stack of old newspapers, could I also take those and the large roll of used canvas you had stuffed in the back corner of your store plus I saw two barrels of used rope. We'll also need six bags of lime, a gross of clothes pins and a small can of black paint."

"Ma'am, I'll give you the fat and a bucket of lard if you'll make me some soap when you make your own. I'll also buy any eggs and butter you might have left over. I'd be plumb tickled to get rid of that old canvas and the newspapers and the rope, I'll even throw in the barrels that they're stored in. I'll give you those for free just to get them out of here." Jonah told her.

"Wonderful, but I don't plan on coming into town anytime in the near future. That's why we loaded up on supplies. How will I get the soap, butter and eggs to you?" Mary wondered.

"I make a run through the ranches every Monday morning to pick up milk, eggs, butter, meat and anything else they want to trade. I can pay you cash for what you sell me or we can take it out in trade, your choice."

"Mr. Clark, I noticed that you don't have any ladies dresses for sale here. I am a really good seamstress. If you will furnish the material and the patterns, I will make you five dresses every week that you can pick up when you get the soap, eggs and butter. I will take it out on trade. If you think it a fair deal, I'd like for you to bring me out some quart and pint canning jars equal for the supplies I will provide. Does that sound fair?" Mary asked him.

"Olivia! Come over here, we got us a lady who's going to make us dresses each week that we can sell!" He turned to give Mary a shake of his hand, "Miz. Murphy, you got you a deal. You just tell me what you want each week when I pick up the stuff and I'll bring it to you the next week. Jumping jeehosephats! Am I glad you came to Pine City!"

"We're heading over to the resale shop now for some much-needed clothing. Just put everything in the wagon out front and we'll be back shortly." And then Mary left the store and headed for the Resale store hoping she would find the clothes they desperately needed.

The children's eyes were huge. They had never seen so much ordered or bought at one time before. This lady was buying out the store!

The sign above the door on the store read 'Used and Clean Clothing'. Mary hoped it was also reasonably priced. She found the store owner as soon as they entered. "How much is the clothing you sell?"

"Well we have children's sizes, each piece sells for five cents each except the socks, they're two pairs for a penny. The shoes are ten cents each pair. For adults, the clothes are the same price, but the shoes are fifteen cents. Would you like to buy anything?" She seemed so hopeful that she did indeed have paying customers.

Mary gave her a huge smile and asked her to show them to the boys' section first. She found the right size for Chris and Cam and told them to pick out two pairs of pants, three shirts, three pairs of long johns and a pair of short johns. She wanted each of them to get a pair of suspenders, a nightshirt, four pairs of socks, a hat and a pair of shoes. They were thrilled! They dug in without being told twice!

She and the sales lady found the sizes for the two little boys and they enjoyed picking out the pants and shirts and a nightshirt they wanted, and they even found them hats and shoes. Then she picked up a pair of pants for Kit and a shirt, two pairs of long johns and pair of short johns. She took them all to the girls' section and helped Kit choose two dresses and a pinafore that she could wear with either one of the dresses, four pairs of socks, three pairs of bloomers, shoes and a bonnet and a nightgown.

43

Then they all followed her to the adult section, and she picked up two pairs of pants, three shirts, socks, long johns, short johns, a hat and pair of shoes for Cade. She sure hoped she had the right size!

Even though, the children felt they had bought out the store, her entire purchases didn't total over four and a half dollars. Mary felt like she had hit a gold mine in the clothes, and the children loved holding their bundles of clothes. They left to settle up with the General Store and Jonah had most everything loaded into the wagon. He told her they would bring the rest of her order out to her sometime today. Mary paid him and her purse felt a lot lighter! She still had some of her money, but she felt like she had made some very good purchases. She picked up six peppermint sticks and paid for them and left smiling.

The children couldn't remember a time they had been given candy. They savored it all the way home. They didn't talk very much, but they smiled at Mary and at each other as they traveled the road to the ranch. Mary felt like Lady Bountiful providing so many luxuries to her little family. She hoped Cade would feel the same way as the children did! She couldn't wait to get home and start cooking the roast, making bread and getting the chicken coup and pig pen built. So much to do and so little time!

CHAPTER 7

When they arrived back at the ranch, Mary told the boys to take some sticks of firewood to the barn to place the lumber on when it arrived. If they left it on the ground, it could warp. She then told them to make a tool bench in the barn for her tools and Cade's, she showed the boys how to nail in two nails and hang up shovels, rakes, the scythe, hoes and any other tools in the barn. She used the axe to cut the handles off the two shovels she had bought for Cade and Cooper and asked them to dig a trench from the house to where the garden would go. They loved using their new shovels and started digging in the dirt with a vengeance! She gave Kit a small scissors and asked her to cut some of the newspapers into small squares they could use in the outhouse. She was to put the squares in an old cigar box Mary gave her. She sat down at the kitchen table and happily measured and cut the paper.

Mary dug around in the wagon and came up with the roast and put it in the oven in a big roaster she had unearthed. She also started up a batch of bread making five loaves hoping that would get them through for at least two days. She also put the fat that Mr. Clark had given her to simmer and melt the fat down to tallow. She then emptied both the fireplace and the ashes in the cook stove into a bucket and filled it with water to make the lye she would need for the soap. She changed into a pair of her husband's pants and one of his shirts and went to help the boys make a chicken coup and a pig pen.

After hanging as many tools as they could, they arranged the rest of them on the tool bench. They even had room to put a shelf under the top and it was here that they put the kegs of nails. The boys unloaded the chicken wire, tar, roofing paper, mesh screen, canvas, rope and the barrels they were in and the stack of newspaper, at least the pile that Kit wasn't using. They put it all in the barn. Mary staked out the area for the chickens and the pigs. By then, the men had arrived with the lumber, barrels and right behind them came the wagon with the rest of their supplies with the chickens, pigs and cow. For the next hour, they unloaded the lumber and put it on the logs in the barn. They staked out the cow in the corral and put the pigs in one of the stalls in the barn. The chickens they left in the crates. Jonah had sent her two crocks to fill with butter, a crate for the eggs and a wooden box to put the soap in. The material and patterns were in a bundle that they placed in Mary's arms. Mary had them unhook the mules and turn them loose, but left the wagon beside the house to unload later.

She had the boys bring her eight 2" x 4"s. She nailed one to the barn wall about eight feet high. She had the boys hand her 2 x 4's one at a time and she nailed them together until they formed a frame 12' x 12' and eight feet tall. Then she had the boys help her unroll the chicken wire and attach it to the 2 x 4 frame. They even covered the top so the chickens couldn't fly out or any animals climb in.

"That looks good, Miss Mary, but there's no door and how do we get the chickens in the pen?" Cam asked her.

"That's only half the pen, the other half will be in the barn so they can get out of the rain or the cold. The door will be there, and we'll build a door for them to enter the yard. Help me build the pen on the inside just like we did this one. But first get one of the doors from your root cellar. We'll use it for the door to the chicken coup.

I have to go check on your sister and the bread." Mary told them as she walked out of the barn smiling.

Kit had cut enough squares to keep them in paper for quite a while. Mary punched down the dough for the bread and set it to rise one more time. She checked on the tallow and it was melting nicely. She asked Kit to come help them in the barn and they were back to build the rest of the chicken coup. Kit was very helpful handing them nails and even in helping the boys carry the boards. Mary used three of the hinges to attach the door of the cellar to the chicken coup. Then she took a small saw and cut a hole in the side of the wall into the outside chicken coup. Using small 1" by 2" boards they made a frame for the piece they cut out of the wall. Mary fixed it with a wire they could attach to the board and it would hang keeping the small door open for the chicks to go out. At night, they would just unhook the small door and it would close until they let them out again.

They brought the chickens in and turned them loose. Mary then helped the boys use the empty crates to make nests for the chickens to lay their eggs in. She even fashioned a feeding trough by using 2 by 4's and putting a small square on each end. It stood up and they could fill it with chicken feed. She used the two inch high barrel end for their water. The boys and Kit brought down enough straw to fill the nests and they were done. The boys were impressed; it seemed that Mary did indeed know what she was doing!

Mary ran back inside to put the bread in the oven and came back to work on the pig pen. She had the boys cut the 2" x 4's into four foot lengths. Using the four foot lengths they built a large rectangular frame and then stretched chicken wire around the entire frame. They didn't need to cover it, because pigs can't fly, or so Mary told the boys laughing.

She used the two half cut barrels and put a piece of 2 x 4's on each end so they wouldn't tip over and ended up making them into troughs. One was for the food and one was for the water. She also cut off the very bottom of one of their large half barrels and set it in the pen as well.

"Go get the pigs and let's turn them loose! I'll get them some water." Mary told them. Each of them grabbed one of the squiggly little pigs and carried them laughing to the new pig pen. They decided to name them Bacon, Hammy and Sausage!

Mary left them admiring their handy-work while she went and took the bread out, turned the tallow off and cut up enough potatoes and carrots to feed an army. She placed the vegetables into the oven with the roast. It smelled very good, and Mary hoped that her first dinner with the family would be a good experience. She brought a bucket of potato peels and carrot peelings out to the pigs and chickens. The children loved watching the chickens and pigs gobble up the scraps.

"Boys, we still have almost two hours of daylight left. We need to unload the wagons, but I don't want to put it in the cabin until there's a wooden floor to keep it dry. So...are you all up to starting on our wood floor tonight?" She asked hopefully.

"Lady, my doubts about you knowing what you're doing have left. You just tell us what you want us to do, and we'll do it. We're as excited as you are about the changes you're making in our home and ranch." Chris told her smiling. Impulsively, Mary hugged the three children and kissed the top of each of their foreheads, and then told them to start bringing her some 2 by 4's so they could begin the frame of the floor.

Mary moved everything in the area by the back door to the other side of the room. As the children brought in the 2 x 4's, she laid them down making three rows of parallel lines to each other. Then she had them start bringing her the 1 x 12 planks. She nailed them to the frame and it didn't seem like it took them very long and the entire area was done. Then, she had them help her unload the wagon and place everything on the wooden floor. Some of the kegs were so heavy it took her and the two boys to carry it to where it could be placed. Finally, they hooked up the mules to the wagon and put it back to where it belonged.

Cody and Cooper had almost dug the trench more than two-thirds of the way to the garden. Mary praised the two little boys and kissed them on the foreheads. They beamed under her praise and came into wash up for dinner feeling very proud of themselves. Mary saw the outline of her new husband coming in from plowing all day. She hurriedly grabbed the clean sheets, blanket and pallets off the clothes lines and went into the house to change out of her pants and shirt and to remake the beds.

Cade had had a very long day. His back hurt from pushing a plow all day and breaking up a never ending stretch of ground. He wondered how Mary fared with his children and how her shopping expedition went. He almost walked by the chickens before he stopped and did a double take. Where in the hell did the coup and the chickens come from? When he went into the barn, he was greeted with the sight of a very contented cow munching on straw in one of his stalls. His anger grew. How much money did she spend? Then he saw the wood all neatly stacked up against the wall of the barn. That's when he lost it! Just who and what did she think she could accomplish buying all this stuff. Cade knew he would never be able to repay the loan for all this lumber to start with. It was all going back, by God! Just wait until I get my hands on that tiny little neck of hers!

His anger lasted until he opened up the back door and smelled the food she was putting on the table. Lord he was hungry and the food looked and smelled wonderful. Maybe he should wait to yell at her until they ate dinner. That's when he realized that he was standing on a wooden floor rather than the dirt floor he left with that morning. His roar almost made Mary drop the bowl of vegetables she was carrying to the table. I guess he doesn't take too well to surprises; Mary thought and then turned to look at her husband with her hands on her hips. If he wanted a battle, then a battle was what he would get!

"What in all that's holy have you been doing today other than spending enough money for two ranches? I don't have the money for the animals or the lumber, I don't know what all else you have been buying, but it goes back to where it came from! If it was good enough for Cate, it should be good enough for you!" Cade almost bellowed he was so mad!

"Now see here, Mr. Murphy! You said you didn't care what I spent my money on this morning! I used your tab for just food and the supplies I will need to make it. Everything else I was able to buy with the cash I had from the sale of my home and my mother's back in St. Louis. I feel that having eggs to cook with and milk for the children to drink, not to mention the butter and cream we can use, are necessities. So are the clothes we bought at the resale shop. I felt the luxury of having a wood floor was worth every penny I spent! I also think your children need beds, not pallets to sleep in. I want a cellar to put all the vegetables I will grow and can for the winter; we will also be able to go into it when there's a tornado or Indians. Your roof leaks. The boys and I plan on putting on roofing paper and shingles to both the house and the barn. We also plan on chinking the cabin and the barn to stop the drafts. And we plan on building a smoke house so that meat won't spoil. If there's something I've done that you don't like, feel free to tell me! Otherwise, it all stays and the children and I will improve on the cabin and barn you built!" Mary told him not backing down.

"We have a cellar; you don't need to build another one. I don't have time to do all you want done! I have fields to take care of or we won't get the corn, wheat and oats in the ground in time to harvest in the early fall." Cade told her with a lot less anger. He appreciated all she had bought with her own money and felt about two inches tall for yelling at her assuming that she had charged everything to his accounts.

"You don't have a cellar. You have a hole in the ground that you covered with a couple of doors. I want a cellar that even you can stand up in if there's a need, and I'll want to get to it from the kitchen with a trap door and stairs. I don't want to trudge through three feet of snow to dig down three feet of snow to get to the cellar!" Mary told him while she put the rest of the food on the table. "I want you to know that your boys and Kit only helped me because I told them what we were doing wasn't going to make you mad. They wanted no part of doing anything that you wouldn't be glad that it was done. I told them that once you got over the shock of so many changes, you would approve of all our work without any reservations. Do you? Have you any reservations about what we do to improve the homestead?" Mary wanted all her cards on the table, if he had any hesitation, she wanted to know now.

Cade swallowed many times and looked again at the wooden floor on half of the floor. He had to admit that it looked nice and it sure would be nice not to have to feel the cold hard earth beneath his feet every morning. Being able to eat eggs would also be a huge boon, not to mention having three pigs to butcher come the fall. He looked at each of his children and smiled for the first time that day. "I didn't know that women could do that kind of stuff. I'm sorry for the way I reacted. I'm really proud of the changes you've made. If there's anything I can do to help when I'm done with the plowing and the planting, I'd like to help make this a better home for all of us. I thank you, Mary, for the generous use of your own money to do so much for us." He hesitated; he didn't know how long Mary might stay mad at him. They were virtually strangers; they had a lot to learn about each other.

He found out that Mary didn't hold a grudge. She smiled and told them all to sit down while the food was still hot. She had made them a feast out of the supplies that their father had provided. They all sat down with astonishment on their faces. Mary had cooked up the roast so it was almost falling apart. Roasted potatoes and carrots sprinkled with brown sugar rounded out the meal with fresh cut loaves of bread that seemed to melt in their mouths.

"I don't know how you helped with all the work on the chicken coup, pig pen and floor and still had the time to cook us up a feast, but I'm starving, and nothing could look better than this. I thank you. We will all enjoy every bite!" Cade told her.

Mary helped fill the plates of the smaller children and cut up their potatoes and carrots and meat. She heard delicious murmurs from all around the table. It was a good end to a very productive day!

CHAPTER 8

Morning came all too early for Mary. She hadn't slept very well in Cade's bed. No matter where you laid down in the bed, you'd roll to the middle and with both Cade and Mary's weight it was enough to have it touch the floor. That bed was going to have to go! After they finished the floor in the cabin, they would begin making beds for all of them to sleep in.

Mary went out with Cade to milk the cow and gather the eggs. She took them both back to the kitchen. She strained the milk with some cheesecloth she had brought with her. The cream went into the butter churn with last night's. She poured the milk into a gallon container with a lid and then put it in the well in the bucket. Inside the well, the milk would get cold and taste better. She fixed up biscuits and gravy and scrambled eggs for Cade's breakfast and made him some roast beef sandwiches to take with him out to plow.

He complimented her on the excellent breakfast and thanked her for the lunch. It had sure tasted good yesterday when he stopped for a break at noon. He wished her luck on her day's activities and left with the ox to continue plowing. Mary made up even more biscuits for the kids and then changed into the pants she had on yesterday and started washing the children's clothes. She had been pleased to see that Cade's new clothes fit him pretty well. He looked good in the dark grey twill pants and plaid shirt with the suspenders. His boots had even fit him!

Chris and Cam came down the stairs wearing new clothes too. They were really proud of them. They liked the fact that they were long enough and big enough to put up with them each growing like weeds! They dug into the biscuits and gravy and loved the scrambled eggs.

"What do you have lined up for us to do today, Miss Mary? After Cam and I chop wood for a while, we'll help you with everything you want to get done. Won't we, Cam?" Chris told her on his fourth biscuit.

"Pa was sure surprised yesterday when he came home to find out we got us some chickens, pigs and a cow! I don't know what was a bigger surprise, the critters or the wood floor! I'm sure glad he wasn't mad at us! I liked helping you yesterday and can't wait until we get the rest of the floor finished so we can start on the beds!" Cam told her taking some more scrambled eggs.

"He was surprised all right! I'm glad he isn't mad about the changes and things we bought yesterday. Today I want to finish the wood floor in the kitchen and in our bedroom. I also want to start making beds first for your father and then for each one of you. I'm not going to stop until; we're all sleeping on feather mattresses and up off the floor!" Mary told them laughing. "We will have to dig out a place for the trap door to be in the new floor. It'll be easier if we do it now so we can reinforce the trap door as we lay the new floor rather than lay the floor and then redo it when we need to put in more support for the trap door. As soon as I finish washing and hanging up all your clothes, I'll start digging in the cellar. You boys can join me, when you're done chopping."

All three of them walked outside together to begin the work for the day. Mary had to put up more clothes lines to fit all the clean clothes. Then she went inside to cut some of her mattresses in half and sew the new seams up with her sewing machine. She wanted them to be ready as soon as the beds were ready for them. It was a tight fit with all the supplies they bought yesterday all piled behind the sewing machine, but she got it done and then started on

54

digging out the cellar for the trap door. She had to stop once to fix the three little ones breakfast and get them started for the day.

Cooper and Cody continued digging a trench to the garden. Kit came and helped her digging in the cellar. They were making some progress. Mary was surprised to see only a few gunny sacks in the cellar. There were no canning jars at all. She was glad she had ordered some from Jonah Clark for the dresses and soap she was making.

As soon as the boys finished chopping wood, Mary sent them with the wheelbarrow down to the creek to get her at least two wheelbarrows full of rocks. She was tired of trying to wash clothes out of a couple of kettles on the ground. She had too much to do to hurt her back bending over the washboard on the ground. She was going to make herself a wash stand before she finished for the day! She and Kit had dug up almost half of the way to the kitchen floor by the time the boys got back. Then she got them digging while she washed the breakfast dishes up and started up a batch of beef stew for supper. She had Kit dry the dishes and they left them on the table clean, but having nowhere to put them!

Then she and Kit started digging down to meet the boys with them digging from both directions, it didn't take them any time at all to get the hole dug. Then they started on the kitchen floor. They carried the table outside and the rockers they had placed in front of the fireplace. They laid down the 2" x 4"s as they did yesterday with one difference. Mary made a brace for where the trap door would be. They slipped the 1" x 12" planks under the cook stove carefully, lifting up first one end and then the other. In little time at all, the kitchen floor was finished with a trap door with two hinges attached to the wall of the cabin and to the door. Mary and the boys were quite proud of the floor. Then they took down their father's bed and went to work putting in a floor in the bedroom.

When they finished with the floor, they moved the table back in and the rockers and moved all the food supplies over to the wall by the trap door. It was much roomier without all the supplies dumped on one third of the floor. Mary called a halt to everyone's work. She cut up some of the ham and with the bread from yesterday, she made everyone a sandwich and gave them cold milk from the well. They weren't used to eating half way through the day and really appreciated the good food.

Cooper and Cody had finished the trench and Mary gave them each a ball pen hammer, she gave Kit the one her husband had made for her son and Cam and Chris used the flat end of their new hatchets to act as a hammer. They started on making beds.

Mary had them begin by making a frame with the 2" x 4" s, then putting the planks for the sides and the top and end of the bed. She made a small ledge inside the planks and cut planks to lie across the middle of the bed. Then she had the boys put nails all around the two sides. She tied a rope at one end and started crisscrossing the rope from side to side. She had Chris on one side and her on the other. It took them little time at all to complete the rope to make some good support and also make it easier for the mattress to lie upon. Once she and Chris were done with the rope, she put Cooper on one end and Cody on the other end to hammer down the nails to keep the rope tight. She put Kit to work on the other side with Cam. When they were done she put a feather mattress over it and slipped on sheets and took a colorful quilt out of one of her trunks. The pillowcases she had filled with grass had been sewn shut and became the pillows on the bed. They were thrilled how nice it looked and couldn't wait to make their own beds!

All afternoon, they made up beds for the children in the same way they had made the one for their father and Mary only these were smaller. The one for Cade was seven feet by seven feet. The ones for the children were three feet wide and six feet long. They still had planks for support across the middle and they still had rope cushions for the mattress. Mary had enough sheets and quilts to make up all five of the beds. The children all had to try them out before they started on the next project. They were thrilled!

Mary took nails and started hanging up their clothes they had just bought on the walls besides their beds. They looked really good and homey hanging there. Then she had Cam and Chris put up a 2" x 4" across the loft edge about four feet high. She had them put in nails all along the top and bottom of the rail. She crisscrossed rope from the floor to the top of the rail just like she did on the beds. Then she had the children hammer the nails down to hold the rope tight. The loft looked a lot more secure with a balcony rail going across it to keep the children from falling over the edge.

While the three little ones were hammering down the nails, she set Chris and Cam to helping her make a kitchen counter for all her dishes and pots and pans. She even attached it to the wall for added security. While she started putting all the pots and pans away, she had the boys make two bookcases with shelves. One went into the room by the fireplace. The other went by the corner of the room where they first put in their floor. Mary rolled the big half barrel over to the corner of the room. She drilled out a small hole in the barrel and bore out a small hole in the corner of the cabin. Then she called Cooper and Cody to help her lay the hose from the garden all the way to the house and into the tub. She filled any leftover hole in the wall with mud to keep it securely in place. She had the boys pour a pitcher of water into the barrel and watch it drain right into the garden! They couldn't wait to take a bath in their new tub.

Mary took two blankets and nailed them to the board above them. She quickly sewed the two edges together making a cozy corner to take a bath in privacy. Chris and Cam decided that Mary knew how to make just about everything! They were really proud of her and glad their dad had picked her to be their new Ma. Before

Cade came home for the night, they all helped to put the dishes away, put all the books on the bookshelf and put towels, sheets and extra blankets on the shelves near the bathing corner. They were all quite proud of all they had accomplished today and couldn't wait until their father came home to see it all.

Mary started making up a batch of biscuits to go with the stew. She also put a basin and pitcher on one end of the kitchen counter so they could all wash up before supper. Mary was just dishing up the meal when Cade came in the back door. He looked with surprise at the finished wooden floor, the kitchen counter, book shelves and shelves covered with towels and blankets. He looked behind the blankets in the corner and had to grin at their new bath tub. It looked to be even big enough for him. A hot bath to ease all his aches and pains would sure feel good tonight. Then he happened to look up and saw the rail and the crisscross of rope making the loft secure. He did a double take at all the beds made up with colorful quilts and the clothes hanging on the walls.

He turned around at his expectant family and smiled. "I can't believe all you got done today! This looks like a completely different house than the one we had just a couple of days ago. I really like what you've done."

Because he smiled, the entire family smiled back at him. He caught Mary's eye and mouthed the words 'Thank you!' to her. She smiled back and told him, "Thank you to you as well, Cade. You worked just as hard as we did. Now come wash up at the counter, there's warm water already poured in the basin. We'll eat as soon as you're done. Children come take your places at the table. Don't start eating until your father sits down and we pray. We need to thank God for all he let us get done today and for all our many blessings in having such a wonderful family."

Cade smiled all the while he washed his hands and sat down to dinner. Things were certainly different then they had been. He wished the house had looked this nice for Cate to enjoy it, but Cate was always happy with the way things were. She did what she needed to do, but never had he expected a woman like Mary to change so much with so little. He was a little in awe of the little lady. He felt he had much to know about his new wife. He looked forward to learning all about her. He felt that things would definitely never be dull with Mary around!

After washing the dishes, Mary started filling the tub in the corner with water. The children and Cade were going to be clean when they slipped between the sheets tonight. She started with Kit in the tub; she washed her all over and even used some kerosene on her hair to kill any lice she might have. When she was finished with Kit, she sent her over to her father to help dry her hair and she started on the two little boys. The tub was so big that they both fit into the hot water. She scrubbed them just like she had Kit. She let them pull the plug for the water to drain and loved as they watched it completely empty the tub. Mary wrapped them both in towels and sent them over to Cade to dry. Then she started filling the tub again with water from the reservoir and refilling the reservoir with water from the well.

Chris and Cam couldn't wait to jump into the tub, one at a time because they both wouldn't fit. While the older boys were taking their baths, she cut the hair of the two little boys and evened out Kit's hair and only cut her bangs. Then she put them in nightshirts and a nightgown that they had bought at the resale shop. They looked cute and angelic lying in Cade's arms. He was so big; he had room for all three in his lap. Mary tucked them all in their new beds and kissed them good night. Cody and Cooper told her 'good night mama' and it brought tears to her eyes.

By the time she had got down stairs, both Chris and Cam were dry and ready for her to cut their hair. Cade started filling the tub and refilling the reservoir while they both got sheared by Mary. It was amazing how much older they looked with the shorter hair. They really looked just like their father, just a lot smaller. She tucked them into sleep just like she had the younger three.

"Good night, Miss Mary. These beds sure feel good. Thanks for showing us how to make them," Chris told her with a grin.

She kissed his forehead and smiled, "Let's just make it Mary, all right? It's too much to say otherwise and since we're all family now, there's no need to be so formal."

"I'd like that...Mary." He rolled over and gave a great sigh of contentment.

By the time Mary got downstairs, Cade had the bath water already for her. She thanked him and didn't need to be told twice to soak in the nice hot water. Cade told her not to drain it, because he was going to take a hot bath too. Mary did just that, but brought over several buckets to make the water hot again. While Cade took his bath, Mary cut out two of the dresses for the General Store. She would start sewing on them tomorrow night. Mary's hair was almost dry as they went in together to sleep in their new bed. Cade's deep chuckle as he lay down and didn't roll to the middle, made Mary laugh as well.

"This bed feels wonderful! I don't know how you did it, but I feel supported even as I feel like I'm sleeping on air! I should sleep like a baby in this bed, thank you again Mary for making beds for all the children. I know it was a lot of work but they sure look great and they really seemed to appreciate it. I've never seen them in such a hurry to take a bath or go to bed!" Cade laughed. "Good night, wife!" And with that, Cade leaned over and kissed Mary good night.

Mary whispered, "Good night, husband!" with a smile on her face and fell into a dreamless sleep.

CHAPTER 9

When Mary and Cade got up the next morning, they both felt pretty good. The bed had given them both a great night's sleep and being clean too, didn't hurt them either. As they walked to the barn together, Mary asked Cade if before he started plowing the fields, he could plow the area for their garden. She knew they would need to start planting as soon as possible to get things grown in the short amount of time they had. He agreed and asked her to mark what she needed plowed. He couldn't believe how big she wanted the garden to be, but he told her he'd get it done before he left for the fields. Mary thanked him and headed back to the house with the eggs and milk.

Breakfast this morning was fried potatoes, ham and eggs over easy with toast. Cade felt like he was eating like a king. She had remembered to make him some sandwiches to take with him, and he left to go plow her garden. Mary started making more bread and to setting some beans to soak for dinner tonight. She thought ham and beans would be a different kind of a meal for them all to eat, and she would make sure that she had plenty of cornbread and freshly churned butter as well. Then she went outside to build her wash stand with the rocks the boys had brought from the creek yesterday.

She dug a hole and using the dirt from the hole and the cellar, she built a stand of rocks using the mud to hold them in place. At the top of the three foot high tower she placed a grill plate she had brought with her. She added a layer of rocks on the outside of the grill to hold it in place. Then she made a wooden rectangular box to sit beside it. She would be able to put one kettle on top of the wash stand to keep the water hot while she washed them using the wash board, then she would wring them out with the two rollers her Ben had fashioned for her. The two rinse kettles she would sit on the wooden box. It was high enough that she didn't have to bend over so much and saved her back a lot of strain. She started a fire in the wash stand to bake the mud and went back in to fix breakfast for the two older boys.

As they ate, she outlined their day. "I want to put a new roof on the cabin today. I will show you how to use the froe and mallet and make shingles. When you go out to cut down some trees for the logs to chop up, bring in a couple of extra logs. It's from those that the shingles will come from. While you and Cam cut the shingles, I'll climb up on top of the roof and use tar to hold the roofing paper in place. Over the paper, I'll nail down the shingles. When we finish the roof, we'll cut the canvas to divide the loft into three small rooms. How does that sound?"

"Sounds real good...Mary. I can't imagine having some privacy from Kit, Cody and Cooper! I'll make shingles until my arms fall off to get that done!" Chris told her with a grin.

"I love our beds, Mary! I've never slept so good, it was like I was floating on air! And I was even warm!" Cam told her as he finished off the food on his plate.

"Good! I hope the walls of canvas make enough of a difference to give you the privacy you need. Why don't you go get some logs, and then I'll show you how to make the shingles? That way I can make breakfast for the three little ones, cut room for a sink and finish the bread up." Mary told them even as she gathered the dirty dishes to wash.

As they headed out the door, she saw that they were wearing their hatchets in their belts. She smiled as she put the bread into pans to rise and wash out the dishes. She ran up the stairs to make their beds and gather up the dirty clothes. Then she started churning the cream into butter. When that was done, she took the piece of tin that they had bought from the General Store and cut it until it made the sink she wanted. Using a thin saw, she cut the opening for the sink in the kitchen counter. She hammered it into place being careful to leave a small hole for the water to drain just like the tub did. She had another job for Cody and Cooper when they woke up.

The two boys were excited to make another trough for the hose and couldn't wait to see water drain to the garden. She had Kit help her make up the beds and collect any dirty clothes. Together they took them outside to wash at her new cook stand. Kit couldn't believe how much fun it was to turn the handles on the wringer. In no time they had the clothes washed and hanging on the clothes lines. Then they returned to make up a batch of cookies to surprise the boys when they returned with the logs.

Mary changed into pants again to climb on the roof. The boys decided that one of them would chop wood for the wood pile and the other would make shingles. Kit would climb the ladder handing Mary the shingles as she needed them. Mary had a piece of cloth that hung over your shoulder with two large pockets at each end. She told Kit to put the shingles in the pockets and give it to her. That way Mary and Kit had both of their hands free to hold onto the ladder and the roof. Mary started up the ladder to the roof with a large container of tar. Chris handed up a roll of roofing paper. Mary wore a carpenter's apron with a hammer and nails in the pockets. She also had a carpenter's scissors to cut the roofing paper. She had used the same scissors to cut the thin tin for the sink. Their progress was slow, but it did get the job done. They stopped for lunch of freshly buttered bread and cookies and really cold milk. They thought they were eating a feast!

They went back to finishing the roof before they could start on the loft. Mary's arms felt like they were made out of lead by the time she was done with the shingles. The roof looked really nice, and they all noticed that dark thunder clouds were rolling in. Mary was so glad that they had the roof on in the nick of time! She went up into the loft and measured how tall the pieces of canvas needed to be and how long. It was easier to measure them in the yard, cut them to the desired size and carry them up to the loft than to try to cut them in the loft. Having cut the canvas, Mary cut a large enough piece to cover the open hole for the cellar and hold it down with large rocks. She didn't want a pond to develop before they started on the cellar. She helped the little boys lay the hose from the house all the way to the garden. They even got to pour the first glass of water down the sink. They were quite proud of themselves of the job they had done!

It took all five of the children to hold the canvas in place so Mary could nail it to the ceiling and to the floor. She curled the ends around a 2" x 4" and then nailed the board to the floor and another to the ceiling. It kept the canvas nice and straight. She put a wall between the two small boys' beds and Kit's and then another wall between Kit's and the two older boys. Then they started on the wall to close the bedrooms off from the rest of the house. By the time they were finished they had a four foot walkway from the doorway of their rooms to the edge of the loft.

Mary cut 'doors' in the canvas and then rolled the doors up to attach them with a canvas strip to tie them to keep them up. When they went to sleep, they would unroll them and enclose the rooms. They were thrilled! Mary even cut two of her trunks in half. She put half of one of the trunks in each of their bedrooms for their long johns, socks and in Kit's room, her bloomers. Each of the rooms looked warm and homey with the colored quilts on the beds and the clothing hanging on their walls. The remaining half trunk, she put in the with the wash tub. Now they would have a place to put the lantern as they washed.

They all helped in putting the tools away and taking down the clean clothes from the clothes lines. They even took up their own clothes to hang on the hooks in their rooms. Mary started on making cornbread and putting the large pan of beans onto cook with large pieces of ham in it. The whole house looked better and smelled really good.

Mary started working on the dresses for the General Store while she waited for her cornbread to cook. She was able to almost finish them before she heard the rain come down. She called to Chris and Cam to go milk the cow and gather the eggs and get all the animals into the barn for the night. She hoped that Cade wouldn't be too far behind them.

She cut the oil tablecloth she had purchased at the General Store to fit the table. The blue gingham looked bright and colorful on the table.   Then Mary started filling up her pottery jars with flour, sugar, salt, pepper, cornmeal and oatmeal. She sat the colorful jars on her kitchen counter. She filled one of two-quart jars with all her wooden spoons, ladles, can opener and large serving spoons, the other she filled with their knives, forks and spoons.   Then she attached her grinder to the end of the counter where she could use it as she needed it.

She washed the inside of the kitchen windows and the bedroom window, too. Then she took curtains that she had had at her home and her mother's and hung the white eyelet curtains over each of the three windows. The rest of the curtains she hung on the kitchen shelves to keep the dishes clean. Never did the Murphy family imagine that their cabin could be so welcome.

Everyone talked as they gathered that night at the kitchen table to eat. Cade appreciated that he had dry clothes to change into when he came home drenched from the fields. The smells made his mouth water, and he couldn't get over the change to his home. They didn't have to put out buckets to catch the water as it dripped through a leaky roof. The kids had shown him their rooms up in the loft and looking at the kitchen and his bedroom with the light eyelet curtains brought a very satisfied sigh from his lips. Mary had sure outdone herself. He couldn't wait to see what she had up her sleeve to do tomorrow! Each day seemed to get better than the last!

Sending the children up to bed and tucking them in, Mary returned to the sewing machine to work on the dresses for the General Store. She was able to finish up the first two and cut out and begin sewing on the next two. She finally decided that she had had enough and headed for the bed. Cade was already asleep and Mary was glad. She knew they were married, but he was a stranger after all. She wasn't used to sleeping with strange men in her bed and Cade was so big, he took up a lot of the bed! Glad she had made the bed extra big to account for his size; Mary settled herself on her side of the bed and fell asleep almost immediately!

CHAPTER 10

Mary dressed in old clothes today to chink the walls of the cabin. She could feel the wind blowing last night with the driving rain. The roof was a welcome addition to the cabin, now she would do the walls and let the garden dry out so they could plant for the next two days. She really thought that she and the three little ones could chink all the walls except the back of the house, because it was the tallest to make room for the loft. She decided to get the boys digging out the cellar while they chinked the cabin. They would be able to use the dirt they took out of the cellar for the mud/clay they put between the cracks in the logs. Mary thought the mud/clay mixture would work pretty well, especially after the sun baked it dry. She gathered several buckets and the wheelbarrow that was Cade's. She made some small levelers to make sure the mud was pushed into the cracks and the surface was level. She was pretty sure that Kit, Cody and Cooper would be able to handle the job.

Cam and Chris were excited to get the cabin chinked and they even liked the idea of digging the cellar. They started chopping wood, while Mary started a vegetable beef soup with the last of the beef. It could simmer most of the day and be really tender for dinner. She would make them some grilled cheese sandwiches to go with it and the meal would be complete.

Kit and the two younger boys were excited to be able to play in the mud! They usually got yelled at for getting so dirty, but not today! Mary assigned Cooper the two lowest rows of logs, Cody the next three, Kit the next three and she took the remainder of rows of logs to chink. Mary showed them how to take a glob of mud and using the leveler spread it out and make it smooth. Cam and Chris took a trip down to the creek and brought back the wheelbarrow filled with clay. Mary mixed the mud and the clay into a gooey mixture and they began. They were all close enough that they could still carry on a conversation as they worked.

"Mary, I saw all those slates you brought with you. What are they for?" Cam asked as he carried up another bucket of dirt.

"I got my teacher's certificate before I married Ben, my first husband. I got the slates so that I could teach our son Benji at home before he went to school." Mary explained.

"Are you going to teach us to read and write and cipher?" Chris asked solemnly. "Ma didn't know how to read very well, and Pa never had the time. We live too far to go to the school in Pine City. I sure would like to know what all those little scribbles on the paper meant."

Mary was thrilled that the children were going to let her teach them. "I would love to teach you all to read and write and yes even to cipher. We'll begin every night after supper while I'm doing the dishes. In no time at all, you'll be reading with the best of them. I'm glad you changed your mind about learning to read and write!"

"Great! I really didn't want to grow up dumb and now we won't have to. Thanks Mary, I'm sure glad Pa married you. I think you know how to do just about everything!" Chris gave her such glowing praise, Mary blushed.

"Trust me; I don't know how to do everything. I just know how to do some things because I used to help my husband with his work. I'm just glad I know how to make things the way we want them to be here. When I lose you two at the end of the month to your Pa, most of the hard stuff will be finished. I will need your father's help putting in the pumps I'm going to order. It'll be a lot easier to pump water, than to tote it from the well. I want one in the barn as well as the house. When the well freezes in the winter, I want a way for you to water the animals in relative ease." Mary went on to explain.

"Imagine that Chris, a pump in the barn! Whatever will she think of next? I can't wait to get started on them with Pa. Remember how much trouble he had carting water from the creek up to the house and the barn last winter? He couldn't get the well water busted up after it froze. It was so cold; the water almost froze in the bucket inside the house. We spent most of our days sitting in front of the fireplace with blankets covering us. We even slept in front of the fireplace! I'll bet the cabin doesn't get that cold this year with a wood floor, a new roof and chinking the walls. Not to mention, how warm those beds are in the loft."

"I hope to make you new winter coats as soon as we get a lot of the bigger jobs done. We still need to put a roof on the barn and chink its walls. It's a pretty big barn; it'll probably take a whole week to get it done. We have to finish the cellar and still build a smoke house and plant a garden. If we have enough planks left, I want to build on a front and a back porch. We'll dig up flowers in the woods and replant them on both sides of the porch and even the outhouse to make it smell better. Although it does smell much better than it did with the lime poured down it and the screen holes in the front and back to let the air circulate." Mary added with a chuckle.

They all worked steadily for the entire morning. Noon found them finished with three of the walls of the cabin and about half of the cellar dug out. Mary washed up and brought lunch outside to eat. She had fixed them some ham sandwiches and poured them each a full glass of the cold milk. It was more than welcome. When they went back to work, Cam and Chris helped. They both stood on ladders to get the top logs and smear them with mud. By the time they were finished, they all looked filthy.

Mary took them down to the creek to wash off most of the mud. They had all been barefoot; thank heavens, Mary decided because she would never get all the mud off them! Mary had them strip at the back door down to their long johns and then sent them upstairs to change into some clean and dry clothes. She took the dirty ones and put some water on the wash tower to heat. She would wash these up and hang them up before she changed her own clothes. But first she decided she would put in a wooden floor to the outhouse.

Mary smiled as she put the small boards into place. She didn't have to cover her nose and mouth as she worked and was proud of the way it had turned out. Then she started washing out their mud covered clothes. She had hung them up in no time and went in to change out of her own. Then she washed up her own, she knew they would need them again to chink the barn, but at least they were clean in the interim.

When the kids were all changed into dry and clean clothes, she told them they were going to play a game while they waited for Cade to come home. She taught them Hide and Seek and Kick the Can. They loved running all over the yard after each other and especially after Mary. They were surprised that a girl could run so fast! Cade came home to find his family running and laughing all over the yard. Mary looked like just one of his kids she was so small.

Mary saw Cade lead his tired ox home. She called a halt to the game and sent Chris and Cam to milk the cow, gather the eggs and help their father put the animals up for the night. Mary took the other three in to wash their hands and get supper on the table. Kit set the table and Mary started on the grilled cheese sandwiches from a frying pan on the stove. It seemed like she had made more than a dozen by the time the boys and Cade came in from the barn.

"Who chinked the cabin? It sure looks like a good job was done by everybody who helped! And look..." He lit a match and there was no breeze blowing through the logs to make it flicker. "You stopped the wind going through our house. It's sure going to be much warmer this winter."

The children beamed over their father's praise. They all sat down to eat and when Mary cleaned up she told each of them to get a slate, a piece of chalk and a piece of cloth from her sewing basket to erase with. On Mary's slate she made the letters 'A' and 'a'. Then she wrote the words axe, ashes, am, and arm. She drew little pictures beside each of the words so they would remember what each word meant.

"Now you try making the letter 'A' and 'a' on your slates. I'll be ready to help you if you need it." Mary continued to wash the dishes and dry them while the children wrote on the slates. The four older children did pretty well, but Cooper just wanted to cover his slate with chalk dust from rolling the chalk on its side. Mary let him have some fun; he was awful little to learn his letters anyway. Cade sat in one of the rockers fixing part of the harness for the ox. He kept one eye on his work and one on the work his children were doing.

"Now, I'm going to write your name at the top of each of your slates. You are going to write it as many times as you can until you know it. All right?" They all nodded their heads. This was fun!

By the time the kitchen was put back to rights, Mary told them that was enough for the day and sent them up to get ready for bed. When they were all ready, she would read them a chapter out of a book she had about being ship wrecked on a deserted island. They were off in seconds and back just as she was sitting down with the book. The entire family listened as she read the first chapter of Treasure Island. Even Cade looked like he was enjoying himself. Then Mary sent them upstairs and tucked them in. She picked up the dresses she had done and finished putting in the hems. Cade couldn't believe how fast her fingers worked with the needle and thread.

"Those are some real pretty dresses you're making. I'd like to see you wearing that yellow one. You'd look real pretty wearing that with your pretty hair and all." Cade told her with a sheepish grin.

"Oh, these dresses aren't for me; I'm making them for the General Store. Jonah is coming out in two days for the five dresses, the extra lye soap I made, the extra butter we have and any eggs we have left over. In exchange for the goods, he's bringing me some quart and pint sized canning jars and lids." Mary told an astonished Cade.

"I didn't know you were making stuff for Jonah, Mary. How do you find the time? I appreciate you trying to save us some money, but you need to not bite off more than you can chew." Cade told her quietly.

"When it gets to be too much, I'll stop. But until then, I want wool to make you all some thick winter coats, two pumps to install with the entire pipes you need, enough goulashes for us all to wear this winter to keep our feet dry, some molasses and anything else I can think of that we might need this summer." Mary retorted without looking up.

"Why do we need two pumps? Isn't one enough?"

"I want one in the house, yes, but I also want one in the barn. When the well freezes, it'll make it so much easier getting enough water for all the animals we have this winter. I know it'll take twice as much work to put in two, but I think it'll make your work a little easier in the long run. Think about it. It'll be you, Chris and Cam putting them in. That's one job I won't be much use at. I'm just not strong enough." Mary told him as she hung up the five dresses all done and ready for the General Store.

"If that's the only thing you're asking me to do, we'll do it. God knows I'd love not to have to break up the ice every morning so we can keep getting water out of the well." He paused, "Mary I sure appreciate all the hard work you're putting in getting the cabin so tight and homey. I didn't want you to think we were taking you for granted."

Mary laughed as she headed for the bedroom, "Every day your children have thanked me for the work they're doing, the clothes they're wearing and the good food I make for them to eat. It's I who should be thanking you for letting me do for your family. They make me feel very needed and appreciated, but it's nice to know that you appreciate me too! Now how about we close up the house, we both have pretty big days ahead of us tomorrow."

Together they went into the bedroom and climbed into the soft, warm bed and in minutes they were both asleep, more comfortable with each other than ever before.

CHAPTER 11

For the next two mornings, they all worked on getting the garden planted. Kit, Cody and Cooper used their planting sticks from the end of their shovels and broom. Chris and Cam needed no such help and helped Mary keep the seeds at the correct depth and length apart. They couldn't believe all the different vegetables they were putting in the garden, nor could they believe the amount she was planting. The garden took up almost a half an acre. They were looking forward to trying all the new vegetables that Mary had them plant. They had never had a beet or popcorn. The times they had tasted sweet potatoes were few and very far between. The herbs that Mary tenderly planted were something new, too. Mary explained that the use of herbs in baking and cooking brought out the flavor of the meat and vegetables. Everything that Mary had fed them over the past week had been wonderful, so they didn't doubt what she told them. If it was good to eat, they were all for planting it.

When they were done with the garden on the second day, Mary suggested that they work on the cellar for the remainder of the day. She didn't look forward to finding a place for all the quart and pint jars that she would be receiving from Jonah today. She had the five dresses ready, the soap cut and stacked in the box Jonah had sent, an entire crock of freshly made butter and over three dozen eggs.

It was while they were working on the cellar that Mary thought she saw the flash off an eyeglass on the hill overlooking their house. She only saw it once or twice and then it was gone. They

74

were so busy that she didn't stop to wonder who it could be watching them.

Mary helped Chris dig for the cellar and Cam took it over by the barn to dump it. They would need it for the chinking of the barn. She was having the three smaller children pick up any sticks they found in the yard for kindling. It was afternoon by the time that Jonah came with his wagon. It already looked filled to the brim with all he had already picked up from the other ranches in the area. He carefully carried in the boxes of quart and pint jars and stacked them in the corner of the kitchen. He looked around approvingly of all the changes he had seen that Mary had already made on the cabin. It was night and day from what it looked like when Cate was here. He smiled, they were very different women.

Mary carried out the five dresses and Chris brought over the box of soap. Cam carefully carried out the eggs and Kit brought out the crock of butter.

"That looks real good, Mary! The missus is going to be mighty pleased with the dresses; she might even keep one of them for herself! You've got almost 200 quart-jars and about 80 pint-jars. There was a little difference on your side so I threw in another large beef roast. I hope that's all right." Jonah told her with a smile. Mary was thrilled because they didn't have any meat for the dinner table and this worked out perfect.

"I couldn't be happier, Jonah. Next week I'd like to trade for a bolt of dark grey wool, a bolt of grey flannel, six blankets and a jug of molasses. Do you think that would be a fair trade?" Mary asked him.

"It sounds good, if there's any difference, I'll throw in another roast or a turkey to make us even. I sure thank you for the goods and I look forward to seeing you next week about this same time." He told her as he climbed into the wagon to head for town. "By the way, the house looks real good. I can see you've all been working real hard to make it so nice. I can't wait to see what you'll have done with the place by next week when I return! Give my regards to Cade!"

"Thank you, Mr. Clark! The children and I've tried to make the cabin more secure and definitely warmer!" Mary told Jonah laughing. She had one hand on Kit's shoulder and the other on Cam's and the children were smiling. Jonah figured they were mighty happy and lucky to get Mary for their new mom.

Getting the jars made Mary want to finish the cellar even more, but she knew that every time it rained, straw was ruined. And once they filled it up this fall, it would have corn, flour and oats stored in the barn as well. They had to do the barn next. It was too important for their wellbeing.

Mary went in to start cooking the roast. The boys kept digging. Mary knew that it would probably take her a good two and half days to put a roof on the barn. It would probably take them at least three days to chink all the walls. They might still have a day or even a day and a half to work on the cellar. Sooner or later it would get done.

It was a long week for Mary and the children working on the barn. She lost Chris and Cam for almost an entire afternoon while they went hunting for game. They brought back a large turkey and a couple of rabbits. It was enough for Mary to make them turkey and dressing for one meal, turkey pot pie for another, a rabbit stew and turkey and rice soup. Cade told her he'd try to bring home a deer sometime this week. Mary agreed they really needed the meat. She couldn't wait to have a smoke house filled so that what to make for dinner was a much easier choice each day.

Mary worked on the barn during the day and sewing on dresses every evening. She still found time to make up another batch of lye soap, churn butter and gather up some extra eggs. They went through all the milk that the cow gave them and they all liked eating eggs for breakfast and loved the cakes and cookies that Mary was able to make with the eggs, milk and cream.

True to his word, Jonah showed up one week later just like he promised. He had the wool, flannel and blankets she ordered and the molasses, but he also gave her another fifty jars of quarts and pints and a large turkey. He told her they sold out the dresses on the same day he brought them in. Anytime she could make them more, they would be glad to compensate her for it.

Mary appreciated the extra jars and wool and flannel, but with all she had to still do to the house and yard, she didn't know when she'd find the time. She did ask if he could bring her two pumps and the entire length of pipe it would take to put them in for next week. If there was any left over, getting meat and jars were really nice and helped them out a lot.

Jonah's eyes didn't miss much. He approved of the new roof on the barn and chinking of the walls. Miss Mary and those children were doing a great job of getting the ranch back to looking as good as it did before Cate got sick. He was glad for his friend, Cade. He needed a strong helpmate to help him raise those five kids, and it looked like he'd found a peach in Mary.

Mary put the wool, flannel and blankets in the house along with the molasses. She planned on making pancakes tonight for dinner along with ham. It was good to get something the children couldn't remember ever having to eat before. She went back out to help the boys in the cellar. They were finally finished digging it. Now they could put in the four 4"x 4"s in the corners and attach the 2" x 4"s to them for the walls. Mary planned on working on the cellar for the next few days to get it done. Then she'd add the porches. If they had time, she'd begin the smoke house. She'd wait until she lost the older boys to Cade to go out into the woods for flowers, mushrooms, wild onions and berries. She would need to build a small cart before they went. Cody and Cooper would get tired coming back, and they would need someplace to put all the buckets of items they picked and found.

In the meantime, they had enough to do to keep them busy from morning till night. Cade had finished the corn and was now working on the wheat. He had been able to plow extra ground this year because he didn't have to watch the children when he was trying to plow. Mary had sure been a godsend! The house had never looked better and neither did his children. They laughed and played and didn't seem to mind doing any of the work that Mary asked them to do. The meals had never tasted better either! She was some cook, everything that came out of that old cook stove melted in your mouth!

With the children's help, they were able to put up the braces and the walls in one day. Then Mary put in the floor and the stairs. The boys started making shelves even while she cut boards for the stairs. She even put up a rail of rope and had the little ones hammer down the nails to hold it in place. They all carried down all the extra jars and supplies to the new cellar. It sure made a lot of difference in the amount of room they had in the kitchen with all of it now located in the cellar. Because they still had time, Mary talked Chris and Cam into making two benches to be used at the kitchen table. She explained that they were building two porches tomorrow and the chairs could sit on it. It would be nice to be able to sit in a chair while she was churning butter or even as she sewed hems in the clothes she was making.

When Cade came into the house that night, he noticed that all the clutter was gone. He saw the two new benches at the table, but he lifted up the trap door to the cellar and taking a lantern, he walked down the stairs and noticed how nice it looked. It was sure a far cry from their old cellar. He liked seeing all the jars to be filled with the garden and the pile of supplies they still had.

When he came up stairs, he was grinning from ear to ear. "Wow! That is sure some cellar you all made for us! I won't mind going into it if we get a twister this summer, and I love having all the clutter gone from the kitchen. Thanks to all my hard working kids and wife, everything looks better now than it has in quite some time."

The children puffed out their little chests from receiving such praise from their father. He didn't give out a lot of praise and it only made his words mean that much more to them.

"What's on your agenda next?" He asked.

"Pa, we're going to put a front porch on the place and a smaller back porch. Next week, we're going to build a smoke house. I hope that we get it done in time to go hunting and put some fresh game in it. There are a lot of us eating and we go through a ton of food around here!" Chris told him grinning.

"That there are, son, that there are. I keep hoping to get a deer, but I'm so busy every day trying to get as much done as I can in the daylight, that I forget about the meat until I'm on the way home. We've been lucky that we've been getting the little meat we have from Jonah for all the goods that your mom has been selling him. You get that smoke house built, and we'll take off a day and we'll all go hunting for enough game to at least make a start on filling it up. How does that sound?" He asked his two older sons.

"Could we really, Pa?! We would really like that." Cam shouted. "Here that Ma, we're going to fill up your smoke house!" It was the first time that Cam had called her Ma. Mary went over and gave him a huge hug and a kiss on the cheek.

"I'd like that a whole lot!" Mary told him quietly. Four of the children now called her mother, mama, or ma. She and Chris were on very good terms, she had all the time in the world for him to call her mother as well.

They started on the porches first thing the next morning. Mary asked the boys when they went to get logs for the firewood, to get two good sized logs for the base of the porch. They had no idea how they would be used, but Mary knew what she was doing so they nodded and headed out on the two mules to bring back the logs they needed.

When they returned, Mary chose the largest of the logs to start cutting it into thirty inch high blocks of wood. She had the boys roll them and placed them in front of the cabin, six in the front and four in the back. Then she took 2 x 4's to attach them together making a frame. She nailed the frame to the cabin itself to give it more stability. Then she had the boys start cutting four foot pieces off each plank. Each plank gave them three lengths for the porch. They had to cut ten planks up giving them thirty boards to lie down and nail down. Then they had to make the stairs. Before she attached the stairs, she had the boys cut and place chicken wire all around the porch. She explained that they didn't want any skunks or opossums making their home under their front porch.

The porch made the whole cabin look better. The kids were thrilled with it and took turns running down it and jumping off the end. Mary went into the house to make them some lunch. They ate it sitting on their new porch. Chris and Cam had even brought two chairs to sit on the top.

They made the back porch that afternoon. It was much smaller only taking up a third of the one they had made in the front. But it gave Mary a place to put her soap molds and wash kettles and butter churn. Here Mary could watch the children run to their hearts content.

She went into the barn and returned with a small board with a hole bored into each end. She had a gunny sack over her arm and three long pieces of rope. She threw one of the pieces of rope over one of the limbs of the oak tree in the yard. She pushed it through the hole and tied a knot. She did the same with another piece of rope. The children were amazed that they had a swing. Kit, Cody and Cooper took turns swinging. She gave the boys the gunny sack and asked them to fill it up with grass from cutting the front and back yard. Mary then proceeded to cut the grass so that it was again short enough not to house any hidden snakes in it. It was also enough grass to fill the sack. She threw another rope over another limb and tied it to the bag. She told Chris and Cam to run and grab hold of the bag. They did it and laughed so hard they couldn't believe how much fun it was. Chris turned to Mary and hugged her.

"That was a great gift...Mom. Thank you from all of us!" Chris told her smiling. Mary hugged him back with tears in her eyes. She walked back to the house to churn butter while she watched her children play for the first time in their own yard.

CHAPTER 12

When Jonah came this week, he couldn't believe the difference the porches made to the house. He could see that they were working on building a smoke house. Mary had Cody and Cooper digging the pit for the wood. She, Cam, Chris and Kit were making a frame for the building. It had 4" x 4"s in each of the corners and they had been dug down about three feet into the ground so they were solid corners. Then they were connecting 2" x 4"s to the four corners at the top and at the bottom. Jonah saw the stack of planks she had waiting to put up the walls and the roof. He was impressed. Mary seemed to know what she was doing and she was setting them up real good to his way of thinking!

Mary stopped the work to get the pumps and pipe unloaded. She couldn't wait to get them put in. She spent a lot of time pulling up water from the well to wash clothes, water the stock and keep the reservoir filled. It would sure save her and Cade a lot of time! Jonah also gave her another jug of molasses, a roast and a keg of nails.

"You've been making so many changes around here; I figured you'd need them sooner or later! I hope that's all right." Jonah told her as he also handed her another bundle of material to sew into dresses, an empty box for the soap and a package of fat for tallow, some more crocks for butter and a crate to put eggs into. "What do you want me to bring you next week?"

"Jonah, everything you bring us is manna from heaven! But I have a strange request for the next few weeks." Mary began smiling. "Cade needs a horse and so do the two older boys. I really don't know who to ask about a horse big enough for Cade to comfortably ride out to herd his cattle. He'll...no...they'll all three need used saddles and horse blankets, not to mention a curry comb, a brush and probably a couple of sacks of oats. How much do you think the horses will cost? And also, I'd like Cade's to be a stallion and the horses for the boys to be mares. That way they can breed them and start their own horse herd."

"That would sure be nice for the boys and Cade, Miss Mary. Let me see what kind of deal I can make with the livery. I know they get horses and saddles all the time. I should be getting a pretty good deal. How about I try to bring all three next week when I come, and we'll figure out how many weeks' worth of goods it'll take you to pay them off? That way they'll have them to do the cattle and any other thing they have to do." Jonah told her with a twinkle in his eye.

"That would be wonderful! They won't be able to get over it! I can't wait for next week to come to see the look of surprise on their faces!" Mary was smiling from ear to ear. Wait until she told the boys! She waved Mr. Clark off in his wagon and put the food stuff on the kitchen table and the two pumps and pipe in the barn. She needed to really get this smoke house built now. With all three on horses, they should be able to get game a lot easier to fill it up with!

It took Mary and the children almost all week to get the smoke house done. They had to start weeding the garden and with it being so big, it took them the better part of two days with all of them working. Cade told them he should be done with all the planting by the beginning of next week. Mary couldn't wait to see his face when he would see the horses.

She even took off one of the days to get four more stalls ready, three for the horses and one for the female ox Mary was going to work on next. Two oxen and a team of mules should make getting in the crops that much easier, not to mention that they could breed them and raise oxen, too. She was pretty proud of the way the homestead was looking. She couldn't wait to get flowers for the porches and start picking berries. She hoped to find some wild rhubarb and strawberries in the woods. There were also some herbs she wanted to look for to dig up and plant on the side of the house. In order to go berry picking, she needed to make a cart. After they finished with the smoke house that was exactly what she decided to do.

Chris and Cam went hunting as soon as the smoke house was done. They wanted a start on getting some meat to fill it up. Mary with the other three children started making a cart. She took two of the wheels she had bought and made a three-sided box that would fit over the axle that attached to the wheels. She put down two 'legs' on the end, so that when the cart was at rest it stayed level. She also put on two longer handles to push and wheel the cart around. As soon as it was done, she gave all the three children a ride around the yard. They loved it and couldn't wait to go out into the woods to get berries.

Mary had finished the five dresses, soap, butter and had the eggs stacked in the crates long before Jonah came on Monday. She had been able to make a coat for Cade and start on one for Chris. At the rate she was going, it was going to take her over a month to get coats for all of them made, but it was going to be worth it. They were thick, warm and with the wool almost waterproof. She planned on putting some rabbit fur around the hood of Kit's to make it a little more feminine.

The boys brought back a deer and were thrilled! They needed Cade's help to gut it and cut it up for the smoke house, but they couldn't wait to get it done. Cade got home early from planting and all three were in the yard when Jonah's wagon came up the lane with three horses tied onto the back. He was grinning from when he saw the puzzlement on Cade's face and the look of longing in the older boys at the horses. When he untied them and gave them to Mary and then pulled out three used saddles, reins, horse blankets, a curry comb and brush, their eyes kept getting bigger and bigger. Then he unloaded the two large bags of oats.

"Congratulations, Cade! You and the boys are the proud owners of these three horses, complete with saddles, thanks to Mary's trade with me. It'll take her almost six weeks to pay off those horses, but in the meantime, you'll have horses to herd, brand and feed those cattle of yours. What do you think of them?" Jonah asked an astounded crowd. The boys were yelling and laughing and Cade just looked at Mary almost with awe in his eyes. Then he did a very uncharacteristic thing for Cade to do. He walked over and picked up Mary and swung her around and around. Then he kissed her in front of the children and Jonah! To his surprise, she kissed him back!

Cade was in a state of shock. Never had anyone done anything this nice for him before! And to get a horse for his boys, too, was almost too much to take in. At that moment, he loved Mary just for the changes she had made to the ranch and in the children and especially his life. He had felt a thrill all the way down his spine when he had kissed Mary. It had been a long time since he had been with a woman. Cate had been sick a long time, and he would never cheat on his wife with another woman. Every day, Cate's memory had faded a little more and when he thought such thoughts, it was Mary's smiling face he saw in his dreams at night.

"Well, say something, Cade! Do you and the boys like my surprise?" Mary asked still holding onto Cade's strong shoulders where he had spun her around and kissed her.

"Mary...my Mary...I don't have any words to tell you how much the horses mean to me and the boys. Thank you...for the horses, for everything." Cade told her and hugged her to him again. "Thank you Jonah. Having the horses will make herding those cattle a whole lot easier! I just never imagined..." His voice trailed off as he went over to really look the three horses over. The stallion was roan colored with a darker mane and tail. He was tall, plenty big enough for Cade to ride him without worrying about hurting him with his weight. The two smaller mares were already in love with the stallion. One was a dapple gray with black spots on her hind quarters; the other was a chestnut brown with a lighter colored mane and tail. They looked to be in excellent health. The saddles and all the gear were used, but they didn't care. He gently stroked the face of the stallion, and he noticed that each of his boys had chosen which mare they preferred. Chris chose the grey and Cam chose the chestnut.

Jonah loaded up his bounty, told Mary she'd be paid off in five weeks and took off down the lane chuckling at the happy family he had just left behind. He had done some major trading to get the livery owner down to his price, but the extra haggling had been worth it to see the look on Cade and the boys faces.

For the time being, they put the three horses in the corral with the cow and the mules. Mary asked them to take care of the deer. When they were finished would be time enough to pamper and get to know the new horses. Kit, Cody and Cooper were glad they got the horses, too. They liked seeing their father and brothers so happy. Cade asked the three children to gather some wood for the smoke house. They were only too happy to help. Mary headed up to the house to begin dinner preparations.

She was stopped about half way to the house with a quiet question, "How did you know?" Cade asked her softly.

"Know what?" Mary was puzzled.

"How desperate we were to get horses to tend to the cattle for starters...It's an almost impossible task to rope and hold them down to brand them on foot. I've been borrowing a horse from our neighbors to the south of us to get it done. Now I won't have to. I repeat, how did you know? I've never said a word." Cade told her.

"You didn't have too. It was like everything else around here. It was something you needed to help make the ranch a better place to work and live. I was glad to be able to find a way to get it done. Mr. Clark was good enough to let me have the horses first and pay for them in the weeks ahead. They will more than pay for their keep just in helping you finish your work a lot sooner." Mary told him. "I am going to remind you of the two pumps we will need to install and the day of hunting for the boys you promised. The other children and I are planning to take the cart we made out to gather some flowers and berries in the woods. The little ones are looking forward to riding on the cart on the way. I hope to pick lots and be able to make us some jam and berry pie. Do you like berry pie?"

"I like everything you make, Mary. You are the best cook I've ever had the pleasure of tasting. There isn't anything you've done that I don't like. It's been so long since I've had a berry pie; I've forgotten what one tastes like!" He laughed, "But I can promise you that if you make it, we'll eat it!"

"Sounds good, I just have about an hour to finish supper for tonight. You and the boys can tell us what you're going to call your new mounts. You'd better take off, the children are waiting..." Mary's voice trailed away. She was surprised when Cade kissed her again and then turned away to tackle the deer. With a sigh, Mary headed toward the house. It had been a very good day all things considered!

CHAPTER 13

Dinner was a noisy and lively affair. Everybody was talking at once on what to call the horses. Kit told them they needed to give a name to the ox; too, after all they had named the three pigs, Bacon, Hammy and Sausage! Cody told them they should call the ox 'Babe' after Paul Bunyan's blue ox that was named Babe.

"That sounds real good, Cody. Babe is just the name for that ox. What do you think, boys, what do you want to call your horses?" Cade smiled the entire meal. It was the first time that Mary had made them spaghetti and after they got the hang of rolling the noodles on the fork, they dug in and loved 'getti', as Cooper called it!

"You know how the grey has all those darker spots on the hind quarters? Well, to me they look like freckles. I thought I'd call her Freckles. How does that sound?" Chris asked them.

"I like it. How about you Cam, what are you going to name the chestnut mare?"

"I'm thinking she's the color of honey right out of the hive. Do you think Honey would be all right to call her?" Cam asked.

"It sounds good, Cam, real good! Now I have to think of a name for mine. Do any of you have any suggestions?"

"It's an awful big horse and it is a kind of red color. Why not call him Big Red?" Mary suggested.

"Big Red? I like it! Big Red, Freckles and Honey will be their names." Cade announced.

"What 'bout the cow? It don't got a name." Cooper said through his mouth was full of 'getti'!

"Can we call the cow Daisy?" Kit volunteered. "I like flowers and milk...so, what if we call the cow a flower's name?"

"Daisy it is! We don't have to name all those chickens, do we?" Cade teased.

The entire family laughed at the idea of naming all their chickens. They all pretty much looked alike and it would be very hard telling one from the other!

"What's on the agenda for tomorrow?" Mary asked. "I thought I'd take Kit, Cody and Cooper out into the woods in the cart to dig up some flowers for the end of the porches and to pick some berries if we can find any."

All three of the children cheered, they couldn't wait for another ride on the cart and picking berries and digging sounded very good to them.

"Well, I thought me and the older boys would take our horses out and try to get us some game to fill that smoke house. When we come back after we get it ready for the smoke house, we'll start and tackle one of the pumps. We'll work on the other tomorrow or the next day. But I will promise you, we'll get those pumps in before we start branding and rounding up cattle. It'll be nice to put our horse away each night and only have to pump some water instead of hauling it up from the well." Cade told them all. Chris and Cam were very excited about being able to spend the day with their father and their new horses.

"Sounds like a very good plan. I know you'll need the rifles for hunting, but would it be all right if I take the shot gun with me? Bears like berries, too, and I wouldn't like to encounter one and not have a way to protect the children or myself." Mary asked them.

"You take one of the rifles with you, Mary. That way if you have to fire it, you won't land on your backside! It packs a powerful whollop when it's discharged. The boys have landed several times before they got used to it. I agree that you should never go into those woods without being armed. I sure don't want anything to happen to you or any of my children. The boys and I will use the other rifle and the shotgun." Cade smiled, "We might have to look into getting another rifle when we go shopping for supplies at the end of the summer. Start a list Mary of all we'll need to get us through the winter. If we add to it as we think of it, we have a lot less chance of forgetting anything important."

"Sounds good, I'll set the tablet on the mantel so that if you come up with something we need you can write it down, too." Mary told them as she started clearing off the table. "Get out your slates, kids. We're going to have some new words to learn today!"

Without another word, the five got up and gathered up chalk, cloth to erase and six slates. Eagerly they sat back down at the table. "First word of the day is 'horse'. Now let's list all the items we need to take care of a horse."

"Saddle!"

"Oats!"

"Blanket!"

"Water?" Cody added.

"Definitely, water!" Mary told him. As each word was mentioned, Mary wrote them on the slate she was holding. Then she wrote, Big Red, Freckles and Honey. "These are the names of your horses, boys. Let's write all of these words on your slates." While they struggled making the letters on their own slates, Mary got out a basin to wash the dishes while she helped the children. Cade had three bridles he was working on in one of the rockers.

"Now, erase the slates and write me a sentence using the words we've already learned and the words of today." Cooper just colored his slate, but he did make the letter C for his name!

Cody wrote 'I like horse.'

Kit wrote 'He rode the horse.'

Cam wrote 'I love Honey.'

And Chris wrote 'Ma got us horses.'

"Excellent! I love your sentences. Now practice writing your names and Cam and Chris practice writing your names and the names of your horses." With smiling faces they bent to the task. Mary finished up with the dishes and told them it was time for the story to be read before they headed up to the loft to sleep. They rushed to get into their nightshirts and nightgown and settle back on the floor for Mary to read to them. They were in a very good part of Treasure Island. Pirates had come to the island!

By the time, Mary and Cade had tucked the children into bed, they had some time before they, too, headed off to bed. Mary sat sewing on one of the coats she was working on for the children. Cade appeared deep in thought.

"Mary...how do you feel about me?" Cade asked her quietly.

"What do you mean, Cade? You're my husband. How do you want me to feel?" Mary answered cautiously.

"I know you loved your first husband and I certainly loved my first wife. I never thought that I could feel anything for another woman, but Mary...you've slipped past all my defenses! You're such a capable person. Everything you've done around the ranch or with the children, our lives are so much better than they ever were before. I find myself watching you at work, you're always smiling, always laughing with the children, you make this a joyous place to live. I've never seen my children so happy. Not just because of the horses, but you've made them feel wanted and needed and useful. They're more confident of who they are than ever before. I've watched Chris and Cam with those hatchets you got them. They are amazing! Whether they're using them as hatchets or hammers, their movements are steady and sure. Kit has always been such a quiet little thing and I see her jumping right in to help you and her brothers no matter what they're doing. Then there's the two little boys, they have never talked as much as what they do now. Cody told me he and Coop are important 'cause they can dig and plant and do just about everything! They don't feel like they're too young or in the way. You've made me very proud of the way the cabin, barn, the whole ranch looks." Here Cade hesitated. He was searching for the right words. "Cate was sick for a long time. I loved her and didn't mind taking care of her, but we weren't physical for almost a year before she died. I found myself being lonely even in the midst of all these children. I...would like to renegotiate the terms of our marriage. I am finding it increasingly difficult not to touch you, kiss you, or make love to you. I'm not going to lie to you and tell you that I love you. I don't know how I feel about you, but I do know that it's your face that I see in my dreams. It's your face and body that calls me to it. Say something, Mary, anything! Tell me what you think of all I've said..." His voice dwindled away.

Mary took a huge breath and let it out and said, "Yes."

"Yes? Yes to what, Mary?"

"Yes, to it all! I find myself thinking about you, too, Cade. The last thing I wanted was another man in my life, but I find that I'm drawn to you, too. I like your quiet strength and the way you did what had to be done for your family to survive. You've been nothing but kind and gentle to me and to each of your children. I find you handsome..." Here Mary hesitated before she continued. "I know that I'm not beautiful like Cate was, but I'm glad you think of me. I've been lonely, too. I'd like to become a real wife to you

Cade, if that's what you want, too." She looked up to see the joy in his face.

"Mary, you don't look at all like Cate did. And yes, she was beautiful to me, but then so are you!" At Mary's sudden look at him, "I'm not just saying that to get you to go to bed with me. When you smile, Mary, you light up the whole room. You are the sun to my children and to me. I find that the sun is beautiful especially when it's coming from a little bit of a lady like you. Come to me, Mary. Let neither one of us be lonely ever again." He held out his arms to her and Mary walked right into his embrace. He held her against his pounding heart for several minutes, before he reached down and picked her up in his arms and carried her into the bedroom and shut the door. For tonight he wanted Mary to be just for him, he didn't want to share her with the rest of his children.

Together they undressed each other with trembling fingers and hands. Cade couldn't count the number of times he had made love with Cate, but he felt like this was his first time. He wanted to make it good for Mary. He was already so excited that he was afraid he was going to embarrass himself and finish before he even got started!

Mary was trembling. Cade was so much bigger than Ben had been. He was taller, broader, his hands were enormous. She could just imagine how big he was everywhere on his body. She wanted to be more than just a warm body for him. She wanted to be the one he reached for in the night and in the day, not just because she was convenient, but because he wanted her above all others. She knew it was too soon for him to love her, but she wanted that too. Without love, the act of making love was meaningless.

Cade caressed her shoulder and down her back. She was small but she was exquisitely made. Her breasts were full and her waist tiny. She had a backside that while small like the rest of her, was more than enough for him. Her skin felt like satin. He marveled that the small hands that were able to do so much work were so gentle on his skin. He continued to kiss Mary and make them longer and longer. His tongue plunged into her mouth like he wanted to plunge into her body. He picked her up again and laid her on the bed. He covered her body with his own before he burst from the wanting of her.

He entered her slowly and he heard her sharp intake of breath. "Am I hurting you?" He whispered to her sending delicious shivers along her body.

"No, you just feel so good and it's been so long. Love me Cade and let me love you!" Mary told him in a whisper.

Cade needed no more assurance that she wanted him. His body took over and he rejoiced in the feel of her against him meeting him thrust for thrust. When he shivered in ecstasy, he felt her body join his. He held onto Mary for a long time, not wanting to lose the closeness they had shared. He lifted himself off her and pulled her close to him to fall into a deep dreamless sleep. This was his woman and he wasn't going to ever let her go.

CHAPTER 14

This morning was so different than every other morning had been for Cade and Mary. They were aware as never before of each other and what had occurred last night, and they hoped every night from now on! He kissed Mary often as they got dressed and wonder of wonders she kissed him back. They went out together to light the fire in the cook stove and the fireplace and then to the barn to milk and gather eggs. Cade took care of feeding and watering all the animals. He also cleaned out stalls. She finished long before he did, she carried the milk and the eggs in to begin breakfast. Mary hummed while she worked.

She felt needed, wanted and strangely enough, even beautiful! She started a batch of bread and made up enough sandwiches for Cade and the two boys to take with them. She had biscuits in the oven and was stirring up some gravy to make biscuits and gravy. Then she started scrambling eggs to go with it. Mary planned what she would need to take with them as the searched for berries and flowers in the woods and what she would make for dinner this evening.

Cade came in and told her he had started up the fire in her wash stand and put on a kettle of water to get hot so she could wash clothes. Mary smiled at his thoughtfulness. They each did a lot of touching as they passed one another in the kitchen. Mary put her hand on his shoulder as she poured him a cup of coffee and placed a heaping plate of biscuits and gravy before him.

Chris and Cam were up early enough to get through chopping their two hours' worth of wood done so they could go hunting. They couldn't wait to spend some time with their horses and their pa.

"Boys, I'm thinking we should take the wagon with us to put the game in. I'm hoping that we get lucky enough to get a couple deer, several turkeys and hopefully a mess of wild hens. If we see a rabbit, great, but I'm hoping for the bigger game because it all feeds us for more than one meal. I plan on butchering the pigs and a steer this fall when it gets cold enough, but until then we need to fill that smoke house and keep it filled as we herd cattle, brand them, weed the corn, wheat and oat crops and start cutting and gathering grass to fill the barn with. We've got a lot more animals this year and it's going to take a lot more straw, hay and grass to keep their stalls clean and feed them. Are you up to it?" Cade asked with a smile.

"Hell, yes, Pa! Me and Cam have been building muscles chopping all that wood all summer. And Ma has been using our muscles to help her get all the work around here done. You put us to the task and Cam and me will get it done!" Chris told him with confidence. His brother Cam nodded that he agreed wholeheartedly!

As the boys started chopping wood, Mary started washing the never-ending pile of dirty clothes that five children went through in one day, not to mention Cade and herself. It was a nice feeling that her family got to put on clean clothes every day. Mary smiled as she went about her morning. She didn't want to get too late of a start digging and picking flowers or berries. But bread had to be made and clothes had to be washed before they could go. She also wanted to scrub the floor with her wash water in the kitchen before they left.

Her men left with the wagon and with Big Red tied on behind. They promised to come back with meat or else. Mary waved them off, but not before Cade kissed her good bye. Mary was blushing even as she laughed.

By the time she got the three little ones up, the wash was done, five loaves of bread sat on the counter and the floor had just been scrubbed. While the children got dressed, Mary made beds and picked up nightgowns and nightshirts to put under their pillow for tonight. She packed a bag of sandwiches for them and a jar of water. She also made sure that she had the rifle and it was loaded. Just to be on the safe side, she slipped her small derringer into her pocket. She also put the boys' shovels and one for her and a knife to cut off bark for willow bark tea and black root. The willow bark tea would be helpful if and when the children ran a fever and black root was very good to use for colds. She also loaded up several buckets for the berries she hoped to find.

When they had finished breakfast and Mary had washed the dishes, they set off. Mary taught them the alphabet song as they rode along in the cart. Even Cooper was singing with them and by the time they were deep into the woods, he could sing it by himself. They found the flowers first. Their bursts of color in an otherwise green and brown wood were easy to spot.

Azaleas, lilies of the valley, violets, black eyed Susan's and larkspur found its way into the cart. Mary was lucky enough to find wild rhubarb and several patches of strawberries. The children loved picking the juicy fruit and even popping several pieces into their hungry little mouths as they filled bucket after bucket. When Mary declared that they couldn't fit another strawberry into the cart they headed back to the cabin.

They ate the sandwiches that she had made for them on the porch. Mary was surprised when two wagons pulled up into her yard. The first wagon held Elizabeth Graham and her three children, Rose, Dylan and Lily. They looked to be about the age of Mary's three oldest. The second wagon held the Drew family, Ava and her two children, David and Emma. They came to welcome her to the territory and to give her some 'gifts'.

Elizabeth and her three children had two little kittens. They were adorable and Kit and Cody reached out hands even before they learned that they were to by theirs. The Drew's had a little wiggling puppy to give to them. Cooper could hardly hold him, but he was sure trying! Mary was thrilled with the additions to their ever growing menagerie! She asked them all to sit down and she would serve them up some tea or coffee.

"We feel bad that we're only just now coming over to get to meet you. We heard from Cade and the boys this morning as they passed our ranch on the way to hunting, they said." Elizabeth told her in the way of an apology. "We sure hate to think that you think that we weren't friendly or neighborly. We haven't seen the Murphy family looking so happy in several years. Whatever you've done, Cade hasn't been this content for quite some time."

Ava looked around the yard and noticed the new roofs and porches, not to mention the chicken coup and pig pen. "You've got this place looking real nice, Mrs. Murphy. Cade was singing your praises when he stopped by our place to let us know that he had remarried. The boys added their thoughts on the subject and I was expecting you to be walking on water or something!" She teased.

"I'm so glad you came by! We've been so busy with making the cabin and barn more comfortable for all of us, that I didn't even notice the absence of neighbors coming to call. My name is Mary, not Mrs. Murphy. I hope we'll all be friends. I want to thank you for the kittens and puppy. I was going to ask Mr. Clark to let us know when he heard of anyone having kittens they wanted to get rid of or puppies that might grow up to be a help with herding the cattle. You've fit the bill perfectly!" Mary smiled at the two women as they all watched the antics of the kittens and puppy with all the children running around.

They stayed and spent almost thirty minutes before they loaded up their crew and set out for home. They both approved of Mary for Cade. She was real nice and friendly, not stuck up like some in the neighborhood they could mention. Ava thought they should have warned Mary about Diana Scott. But Elizabeth thought that Mary might look little, but if she had done half the things Cade said she had done, she could certainly handle one meddlesome neighbor.

While Mary started washing the berries and getting some jam going on the stove, she poured the rest into jars to seal for future use. Mary loved making food for her family to eat whether it was now or this winter. She also set aside enough berries to make several pies for dinner. She had the children to start digging on both sides of the porches for all the flowers they had to plant. It was while they were planting flowers that they had another visitor. This one wasn't so friendly.

Diana Scott lived several ranches to the south of their home. She and her husband had been 'gentleman' farmers and ranchers. In other words, they paid people to plow their land and take care of their crops. Diana had a maid, a cook, a gardener and a stable boy. All of whom lived on the premises. Her husband had passed away shortly after Cate had died. She had designs on Cade from the first minute she saw him. He was a perfect specimen of a man and he made her mouth water. Her husband was older, had a pot belly and was bald, hardly someone to send her into spasms of contentment. With Howard gone, she thought surely Cade would ask her to come and help him take care of all his motherless children. Of course, the first thing she would do would be to send them all to boarding school far, far away. She wasn't particularly fond of the little bastards. She had been friends with Cate because she was married to Cade. She tolerated her whining to keep in close proximity to

Cade. And today she heard that he had remarried and it hadn't been to her! She was here to see for herself what kind of woman Cade had gotten himself tangled up with. In the back of her mind was the thought that she had gotten rid of Cate, she had gotten rid of Howard and one more person shouldn't be too hard to take care of.

Diana was beautiful and spotlessly clean in a very pretty day dress. She had a driver to the buggy she arrived in. Mary was filthy. She had been digging holes to put her plants in and canning berries. Her shirt was stained and covered with dirt and she was still wearing her pants which were equally as dirty. She didn't mind the way she looked when Elizabeth and Ava had come, but somehow this woman was different.

"You must be the new wife Cade mentioned when he came by hunting with his boys." She began, "I'm Diana Scott. I was a very, good friend of Cate's, God rest her soul. I still mourn her and my late husband, Howard. They both passed away close together. It made Cade and me that much closer. I had even thought that someday soon, we might make it permanent in order for the children to be taken care of properly."

Mary didn't like what she implied and she didn't like the way she turned up her nose at her and her children. She impishly held out her hand to shake the immaculate hand of Diana's with her dirty one. Diana hardly touched her hand and she was rubbing it against her skirt to rid it of any contamination. Mary smiled, "It's nice of you to call, Diana. We've been berry picking and gathered some flowers along the way to put on either side of the porch. The children and I have been busy all afternoon. Would you like something to drink?"

"No...no, I just wanted to welcome you to Pine City. I can see that you're busy...perhaps I'll call again when you don't have so much to do." Diana climbed back into the buggy.

100

Mary waved her away and watched her children. They had been friendly and animated when the Graham's and Drew's were here, but they immediately clammed up when Diana came. They didn't greet her or wave to her as she left.

"What's going on? Why didn't you talk to Mrs. Scott?" Mary asked gently.

"She don't like us, Mama." Kit told her with a sigh.

"She called us dirty little bastards before. She told us children should be seen and not heard." Cody told her with a frown.

"She slapped me when I touched her dress. 'Told me I was ruining it." Cooper told her hanging his head in shame.

"Well, let's make a decision right now. If you children don't like someone, you will not have to wave or talk to them. We will be polite, but then we'll tell them we're too busy to visit right now. That way they'll leave and you won't have to feel bad because of something they said or did. But I will tell you right now, my children can talk and laugh all day long and I won't tell you to go away. I love having my children helping me. We couldn't have picked all those berries or planted these flowers without your help." Mary told them and then hugged and kissed them all on their foreheads. They hugged her in return, they were sure glad that Diana Scott hadn't been their new mother!

Cade and the boys came home excited about all the game they had found and almost filled the wagon with! Cade pulled the wagon up next to the smoke house and he and the boys started skinning and cutting up the animals they had found. There were two deer, half a dozen turkeys and more hens than the smaller kids could count. It would take them the greater part of the day just to get them ready for the smoke house. Cade promised Mary that they would start on her pump tomorrow morning at the latest. He was grinning from ear to ear when he bent and kissed her as they arrived. Mary proceeded to tell him about all the visitors they had received that day. The children proudly showed off the two kittens and the puppy. Chris and Cam loved both of the additions to their little family. Mary asked the older boys to help make them a good place to sleep in the barn. She would give them both saucers of milk to eat after dinner was over.

"I had one other visitor, Cade. Her name was Diana Scott." Mary hesitated, "She told me that she thought that you would ask her to marry you and was surprised at the choice you had made. She told me she was a very good friend to Cate."

She noticed the scowl that had appeared on Cade's face the moment she mentioned her name. "She was Cate's friend not mine. She was over here all the time when Cate was sick. She didn't help cook or clean or anything other than give Cate some concoction she made that she felt would help Cate feel better. She assured us it would help after all she gave it to her husband as well. They both died. I haven't had much time for her since then. I don't particularly like the woman; she's kind of stuck up if you ask me. But if you like her, by all means be her friend." Cade told her.

"Well, I didn't particularly like her either. She gave me a look like I was beneath her. I do admit that we all were filthy. We had picked berries, made jam, played with the kittens and the puppy and were in the middle of planting flowers on either side of the porch. She tried to rub the dirt off on her skirt when I shook hands with her. The three little ones didn't like her at all. They were all smiles when the Graham's and the Drew's were here, but didn't say a word while the Scott lady was here. I told them after she left that they didn't have to talk to her, but they did have to be polite to her. I hope she doesn't come to visit very often!" Mary told him laughing.

"I wonder what she would have said if she had seen you up on top of the barn or cabin putting on shingles?" Cade chuckled. "I don't think she's ever put in a decent days work in her life. She has no idea of what it takes to keep a ranch this size running."

"I'm going to make some berry pies for dinner while you men take care of all this meat. Thank you! This will feed us for many weeks to come!" She kissed Cade, Chris and Cam on their cheeks and left to make the pies. All three men grinned and set to skinning and cutting with new found energy.

Dinner found them coming up with names for the two kittens and puppy. As always, the food was delicious but all of them kept eyeing the pies that sat on the counter. They couldn't remember the last time they had berry pie for dessert!

"I like Tie...bear for my kitty's name!" Cooper told them with his mouth full.

"Do you mean Tiger, Cooper?" Mary asked him while she wiped his mouth.

"That's what I said, Mama! Tiber!" Cooper told her with a grin.

"I think Tiger is a great name for one of the ferocious kittens." Cade agreed laughing.

"You know how the other kitten is all different colors?" Kit said. "I think I'd like to call her Patches. Do you like that name?"

"It fits. I say the second kitten should be called Patches just like Kit said." Cam told her with a grin. It was nice having the children supporting each other, Mary thought.

"What kind of puppy do we have?" Chris asked. "I know the Drew's have dogs that do a good job herding their cattle, but that pup sure doesn't look like a purebred."

"You're right about that. He just looks like a multi-mix, in other words, a mutt!" Cade told them laughing.

"He's my buddy!" Cody told them. "He licks my face and runs after me, I think he likes me!"

"Cody, I think you've come up with the perfect name for the puppy!" Mary told him as she passed out dishes with large pieces of berry pie for every single one of them.

"I did? What did I say?" Cody was puzzled.

"You called him Buddy! Buddy is a real good name for the puppy!" Mary ruffled his hair and gave him a hug before she sat down to enjoy her own piece of pie.

"Buddy! I like it! Can we call the puppy, Buddy?"

"We sure can. I'm real proud of the names you three came up with and how nice the flowers look on each side of the porch." Cade told the excited children.

"Mama says we're her helping hands, papa. Me and Cooper dug deep holes for the flowers. We was sweating by the time we was done, then that old Scott lady came by. We don't like her none at all, do we Cooper?" Cody told the entire table.

"Nope and she don't like us neither! She called me bas...bas...tid and said I ruined her dress. But she lied! She was wearing the same dress today and it wasn't either ruined!" Cooper told the room at large.

"She called you a bastard? When was this, Cooper?" Cade asked him quietly.

"She was visiting Mama. Mama didn't say nothing to her, just looked at her. She wasn't feeling too good, she was in bed." He was told.

Cade swallowed and shut his eyes. He wasn't aware of so much that went on around his own home while he was out working in the field, and Cate had been sick and unable to take very good care of the children. He wondered what else he didn't know about. Maybe it was best just to let bygones be bygones and start fresh with Mary. He'd have to think about it, but he sure didn't like anyone, man or woman, calling his children bastards.

CHAPTER 15

True to his word, the next day found Cade and his two older boys putting in pumps in the cabin and in the barn. He and the boys got filthy, but they were so proud of what they had accomplished. They all filled buckets from the new pump and watered all the animals in the barn and in the yard. Cade found himself wondering why he hadn't put them in years ago. He knew the answer to that, Mary. Cate was happy with the status quo; she never pushed them to get in another house from the sod one. It was Cade who got the windows for the sod house, and he was even the one who suggested the wood roof several years later. Even when they were finally in a cabin instead of the sod house, she never even suggested that they needed a wooden floor or cabinets to place the dishes and pots and pans in. He thought about what she would say to all the changes that had been made around the homestead in the last six weeks. It sure made a difference to the children and to him.

The house was no longer cold and leaked. When the wind blew, it didn't blow through the cracks between the logs. When it rained, it only rained outside, not in the barn and getting the hay and straw wet and certainly not in their cabin. Curtains, a tablecloth, cabinets, shelves, rockers and warm beds had made the cabin welcoming and warm. The children loved their little rooms in the loft and loved all the clothes they had to choose from. Mary kept the cabin and the clothes clean and neatly mended. Buttons were sewn on and tears sewn up so that you couldn't even find the rip, and they always smelled so fresh when you put them on. Baths were a regular occurrence now with someone taking a bath every night. They usually had the three little ones on one night, the older two the next night, with Mary and Cade taking the third night, they all liked feeling clean.

Then there was the food. Cate had kept them fed, but to his knowledge she had never used the kinds of herbs that Mary did. The food was bland but plentiful. Mary's food was delicious; there wasn't anything plain about it. She could make eggs become special. She made French toast and egg in a hole in the bread. She sprinkled brown sugar on oatmeal and mush and buttered the toast while it was still warm so that the butter melted on the bread. There were jam and molasses to put on pancakes. Her biscuits were almost as light as her bread. Even cornbread tasted better with Mary making it. Cade found he liked the variety that Mary made of the meals for them. It wasn't just meat and potatoes. It was a roast with glazed carrots and potatoes and enough gravy to smother it all. Her stews, her soup, her pot pies, they were all delicious. Cade didn't really have a preference, he loved everything she made. Then there were the desserts.

Cate didn't make many desserts. She made them to take to a barn raising or some other place where she was expected to bring several dishes. But Mary made desserts for the family. There were always cookies in the cookie jar. She made bars of oatmeal and raisins that melted in your mouth. Her every day cakes, as she called them, were devoured by every single one of his children and himself. And then there were her pies!

What she could do with a little crust and fruit defied your imagination. She could take peaches out of a can and make a mouthwatering peach pie or cobbler. She went out picking every kind of berry you could think of and then made jam, put up berries for the winter and made them pies. More than one, because one was never enough! She was a woman, Mary was. He found he was drawn to her more and more.

It wasn't just the sex, although that was great, it was the way she went about everything. She made every single one of his children feel special and wanted and needed. That's how she made him feel too. He was more than just a husband, he was her friend. He liked her very much and felt like he was falling in love with her as well. She was sure an easy woman to love, Cade thought.

After almost filling the smoke house and putting in the pumps, Cade and the boys had been working on branding all their new calves and making sure that all their older cattle all wore their brand. That was another thing; Mary came up with a brand that they all fell in love with. She drew a large C and inside the C she drew an M. It stood for Cade Murphy, and Chris Murphy, Cam Murphy, Catherine Murphy (Kit), Cody Murphy, and Cooper Murphy. Or the C and M, stood for Cade and Mary. They decided to brand everything in sight with their new branding iron that Malachi Graham had made in his forge.

Branding calves, cows and horses was sure a lot easier on horses than it ever was on foot! The boys were getting right good at throwing a lasso around the neck of the animal they wanted and then together they wrestled the animal down so they could tie several legs together. By then they were pretty still and they could brand them without really hurting any of them. It was a practiced hand that untied the animal with a twist of their wrist and let it up to go back to the herd. With the horses, they were able to brand almost twenty a day. Even then it was going to take them the better part of a month to get all the cattle, calves, horses, mules, ox and cow all branded. Cade's three hundred herd had grown to almost four hundred and fifty with all the calves that had been born.

Their crops were growing by leaps and bounds. Cade knew that the next thing they tackled was weeding the growing crops. If they got to the weeds now, they could stop them from taking over their fields with them. He saw that Mary was weeding their huge garden almost twice a week. She was also going berry, rhubarb, mushroom and wild onion picking. She was collecting quite a variety of wild herbs she found in the woods. She had oregano, sage, mint, sweet basil and lavender growing all along one side of the cabin. When she made soap for Jonah Clark, she often put some of the lavender into the soap to make it smell even better. Cade loved the way it made Mary smell and he even detected the slight smell on his clothes. He didn't mind, it made him think of Mary even more during the day.

While Cade and the older boys worked on branding the animals, Mary and the three little children weeded and picked everything they could get their hands on. They were learning the kinds of trees in the forest and what they could be used for. Cody was really good at finding willow trees so they could take the bark off several limbs. Kit could find black roots for when they developed a bad cold and Cooper could find sage every time they went out. In May, they picked rhubarb and strawberries, in June they found blueberries, currents for jelly and even more strawberries. Mary found walnut, pecan, chestnut and hazelnut trees and bushes. She marked them so she would be able to find them again this fall. She told them all they could use her nut cracker to break them and help her pick out the meat from inside so she could make them nut bread, pecan pies and oatmeal and nut cookies. Just the thought of all those desserts, had them agreeing to anything she suggested.

Mary was also sewing on the cloth from the General Store and making seven warm coats for them all to wear this winter. She had another list she was making to what she still needed from the General Store for the winter and for what she could trade for. She was a very happy and contented person except for one little thing, or rather one little person. Diana Scott. She came around at least once a week and expected her to drop everything she was doing to talk with her. Mary tried to be polite and stop to chat with her, but she couldn't let her jam or jelly boil over while she sat and had tea. She refused to lose the time she had to sew talking to the woman. Mary was getting very angry at the time the woman expected of her.

On this particular day, Diana came while she was sewing. Well, at least I'm not filthy or wearing pants, Mary thought as she opened the door to let Diana in. She was carrying a plate of her 'special cookies' that she liked to bring over for them to eat. The only problem was the children didn't really like her cookies. Cooper and Cody told her they gave them stomach aches from eating them. Chris and Cam told her not to eat them, but when she was gone to throw them down the outhouse. They didn't want to take any chances that their new Ma would get sick like their other mother had from eating the cookies. Mary had her own reservations about the cookies that Diana made for them. She had even put one in an envelope and sent it to Wes, Lily's husband, back in St. Louis. He worked for the U.S. Marshall's office and he could find out what made the children have a stomach ache when they ate the cookies. She hadn't heard from him yet, but until she did, she was going to follow Chris and Cam's advice.

"Hello, Diana. Come on in, I'll put on a pot of tea." Mary told her already regretting the invitation.

"Thank you, I will. I won't stay but a short while; I know how busy you are. Where is Cade today?" Diana asked looking all around the little kitchen.

"He and the boys are still branding the cattle. They hope to be done in the next day or so, and then they'll start weeding the corn, wheat and oats." Mary told her while she poured her a cup of hot tea.

"I can't help noticing all the changes you've made to the cabin." Diana began, "Cate was satisfied the way it was."

"I'm not Cate, I wanted more and was able to give us more." Mary told her gently.

"Cate was happy without the cabinets."

"I'm not Cate; I wanted to get rid of the clutter. It's cleaner and doesn't look so messy this way."

"Cate didn't want the children to be separated in the loft."

"I'm not Cate and the older boys needed some privacy and so did Kit."

"Cate wanted to see the sun shining through the windows. She didn't like curtains."

"As I said before, I'm not Cate. I like the sun shining through the windows, they're clean and the curtains give us some privacy."

"Cate didn't want any tablecloth. She wanted to see the beauty of the wood."

"I'm not Cate; the table cloth protects the wood of the table and is easier to clean up after meals."

"I heard that you got up on the roof to make the shingles, Cate would never put on pants or get up on the roof!"

"I find that wearing pants is easier to get some things done. The roof in particularly was better for pants than a skirt blowing in the wind. Cate might not have known how to fix the roof, but I do. If I can do it, I will get it done. Cade has enough to do around here without having to worry about fixing the roof or chinking the buildings. Thankfully I had the children to help me get it done."

"Cate would never have let the boys wear hatchets or work so hard."

"I am not Cate. I don't work the boys or Kit any harder than is necessary to get the job done. The children actually like learning how to do things; it's not so boring around here for them."

"Cate would never let them have cats or puppies. They're filthy animals and I'm sure they'll make them sick!"

"For the last time, I am not Cate. I don't do things like Cate, and I think all children need animals to take care of and learn responsibilities. And now, I hate to rush you, I really need to start weeding the garden." Mary paused, "Unless you would like to stay and help?"

"I'll be taking my leave, it was nice...visiting with you...Mary. You and Cate are so different; I don't see how Cade could have made the choice to marry you with other people around that he could choose." Diana told her with a frown.

"Diana, I'm a little tired of you comparing me to Cate. I'm also tired of you telling me about the other women Cade should have chosen. I am his wife, and I intend to stay his wife." Mary took a deep breath, "Perhaps it would be better if you didn't visit me when what you really want is to look things over and tell me how much Cate would have hated everything I've done to make things better. I simply don't have the time to listen to you go on and on about what Cate did or didn't like. It is what it is. Accept it or not, your choice. Thanks...for the cookies." Mary walked the surprised Diana to the door and out to her waiting buggy. She didn't wave as she drove off. Then Mary walked back into the house and picked up the cookies and dumped them in the privy. It gave her immense pleasure to see her cookies go down the hole!

She smiled for the rest of the day as she remembered how Diana had left. Maybe now she wouldn't visit any more, one could only hope!

CHAPTER 16

By the end of June, Mary's debt for the horses had been paid. She asked Jonah Clark to bring her a female ox. It needed to be a couple of years old so that they could hitch her to a wagon but young enough to be bred to their male ox. Jonah laughed and told Mary her wish was his command. He liked visiting with her for the few short minutes they had loading up the dresses, soap, butter and eggs. "Are you and the family coming to town for the Fourth of July Festival?"

"I really don't know, Jonah. This is the first I'm hearing about it. What all does it entail?" Mary was intrigued. She had been on the ranch for more than three months and the thought of going to town sounded good to her for all of them. Everyone had worked so hard to get them in great shape that a holiday sounded like a reward for everybody.

"Well, most of the women around bring in picnic lunches for their families, although there are restaurants open to serve food, too. There are games for the children to compete in, stands to buy what-not's and after dark there's a dance and lots of fireworks. Pretty much the whole town and all the ranchers come in for a much needed break. Talk to Cade and I hope to see you and the family at the shindig next week." Mary waved Jonah off and went back to work. Today was a weeding day, and the garden was so large that it took an entire day of pulling weeds and feeding them to the chickens. They loved weeding day, but Mary and the children did not. Thanks to all the spring showers they had been blessed with, the crops and the garden were flourishing. Mary would be picking green beans in about two weeks, having a break from all the work would be welcome.

That night at supper, Mary brought up Jonah's invitation.

"Do you ever go to the Fourth of July celebration?" Mary started, aware that every single one of the children stopped eating to listen to what their father said.

"We haven't in so long, I clean forgot about there being one!" Cade replied. He looked around the table at all his children's longing at the thought of going to town for just such an event. "I think we should go this year, if for no other reason than to show off their new Ma and my new wife. What do you think?"

"I think it would be a great idea! Everyone has worked so hard getting us ready for the winter; we should take a day off to enjoy the summer. I'll make a picnic lunch that's big enough to serve us two meals. I'll bring a change of clothes for us all to change into if we need to, some extra jars to hold water and even some cookies to eat whenever anyone gets hungry. How does that sound?" Mary smiled at Cade. This was going to be fun.

"Sounds perfect, although I ought to warn you, I'm expecting to dance with my wife that night. I don't want to fight off all your eager admirers!" Cade teased.

"You just might be stuck with me for the whole night, Cade. I don't know anyone in Pine City except our family and a few women who've come to call." Mary told him.

"Good. That means I'll have you all to myself!"

"Yippee!" All the children yelled together and they began to plan how best to get ready for the big day.

Jonah brought the ox the day before the celebration. Mary loved her on sight. She was smaller than Babe was, but she looked to be in excellent condition. She couldn't wait for Cade to see her.

"She's perfect Jonah. Thank you for bringing her out today. We're planning on coming in tomorrow for the big bash. So, we'll probably see you and Olivia there." Mary told him.

"That's why I came today; I'm hoping to sell all five of those dresses tomorrow and all your soap, butter and eggs, too. I'll tell Liv and we look forward to seeing you all there." Jonah told her. Mary gave him the measured paper she had cut for each of their feet. She wanted Jonah to order goulashes for her entire family. She also needed some more yarn to finish knitting hats and scarves for everybody. Then she'd start on her list of Christmas gifts for the entire family. If she could trade for them, she'd have a Christmas they would never forget.

Cade and the boys couldn't believe the ox Mary had traded for. Mary explained that Babe and Belle, the name they gave the female ox, could have little oxen that they could keep or sell just like the colts and foals they hoped to get next year from Big Red and the two mares, Freckles and Honey. Cade picked her up and swung her around, "Is there anything you don't think of? Having another ox to pull a wagon in the fall is perfect. We always were borrowing from the Graham's or Drew's to get the extra wagon for threshing or cutting. Belle will be more than welcome!" Cade laughed, "What else are you planning on to surprise me with?"

"Not anything important, just some boots for everyone to wear this winter so they won't get wet feet in all that snow." Mary laughed with him. She didn't want to tell him about the Christmas gifts, because some of them were for him!

The Fourth of July dawned bright and sunny. Everyone flew through their chores and taking care of all their animals. Mary packed enough food to feed an army or at least seven very hungry children and husband. She also packed enough water, clothes and even brought along food for the two mules that had to pull them to town. Everyone was wearing clean clothes; Kit had even agreed to wear a dress and pinafore for the occasion.

Jonah had been right; everyone and I mean everyone had come to town today. The roads were crowded and Cade waved to almost everyone they ran into. Mary was looking forward to seeing Elizabeth and Ava today and of course, Jonah and Olivia. She hoped against hope that she didn't have to spend too much time with Diana Scott. Just the thought of her, made her lose some of her enthusiasm for the celebration. As each child got out of the wagon, Mary pressed some coins into their hands. To Cam and Chris, she gave each of them a quarter. They saw how much it was and gave her a hug and a kiss on her cheek. To Kit and each of the little boys, she gave a dime. They were thrilled and Kit was soon leading them with her to the games they had for the children to play to win prizes. Cade followed them; Mary's arm was through Cade's proclaiming to one and all that she belonged to him. He was proud of his wife and he was going to enjoy showing her off.

The first person they ran into was Maggie McDonald, Brenda's sister. Cade introduced them to each other. Without Maggie, he never would have met Mary, so Cade told her 'Thank you' several times in the course of their conversation.

"I'm so glad to finally meet you, Mary. Cade you don't have to tell me thank you again, I can see how good an arrangement it's turned out to be! I'm so glad! You and the children certainly needed some help and from all Jonah has told me, Mary is a miracle worker!" Maggie told her giving her a welcome hug.

"Maggie McDonald, I could hug you for sending Mary to us. But then I'd have to settle down my wife for hugging another woman!" Cade laughed. Mary noticed how often Cade laughed these days. She must make him happy and that made her very happy.

"Mary McDonald, I was hoping to run into you today. I wanted to tell you how glad I was to get your telegram telling me about

Cade and the children. They have changed my life, and it's all been for the better. Without you, I never would have sold everything I had and traveled so far to meet someone who needed me." She took a deep breath, "I love Cade and the children, I have never been happier."

Cade heard her declaration and picked her up in front of God and everybody at the celebration. He kissed her and whispered in her ear, "I love you too, Mary and I've never been happier in my life!" Mary kissed him back and positively glowed she was so relieved that her love was returned.

"Well, I can see that it was a good decision all around!" Maggie joined in on their exuberance. "I happened to see Chris and Cam a little while ago, I almost didn't recognize them from the way they looked about three months ago! I almost fell down when I realized that I saw Kit in a dress! She had Cooper with one hand and Cody with another hand. I've never seen them looking so good and smiling so much. I've a good feeling that the whole family is happy about the two of you!"

"They are and we are!" Cade told her hugging Mary close to his side. "You should come out and see how things look now; it's an entirely different place to live. Mary and the boys have put on roofs, chinked walls, put in a wooden floor, made a cellar, a smoke house, chickens coups and a pig pen. And that's not mentioning the horses she traded for or the pumps we've put in the cabin and the barn. Why just the other day, Jonah showed up with a female ox, my wife plans on breeding with my male ox. She's about the best cook in the territory! I don't think there's anything that my wife can't do!"

"We'd love to have you come out and see us, Maggie." Mary told her, "Maybe you could come for a meal and stay to chat. I promise I'll stop whatever I'm doing and enjoy just spending time with you!"

"You mean you won't invite me to pick weeds with you?" Maggie smiled at the slight blush that came over Mary's face and neck. "I thought that was a great way to get rid of unwanted guests! Diana has been in a snit ever since Cade married you. She wanted to be the one to marry him. Of course, I knew that Cade had better sense than to give her the time of day, but you sure threw a kink in her wheel when she saw how well you were doing out there. She was sure you'd be running to the hills by now with all those children and everything being in such bad shape. We all had a chuckle when she told us you invited her to weed your garden with her! I don't think that woman has done an honest day's work in her life! I was proud of you even before I officially met you, Mary! You've got spunk that's for sure." She leaned down and hugged Mary and whispered, "Be careful around Diana. I'm not quite sure what she has planned, but she's had her eye on Cade for quite some time. Some of us thought she was only 'friends' with Cate so she could be close to Cade."

Mary looked her square in the eye, "She'll play hell getting him away from me, Maggie, but thank you for the warning! Somehow, I don't think we'll be bosom buddies after I sent her on her way the other day. Would you care to join us for lunch or dinner, I brought enough to serve half the town?"

"I'd love to, but I have boarders to feed at my rooming house. But I promise to come out and visit real soon. And I'll tell you, I don't mind weeding in your garden! I love the feel of dirt beneath my fingers and making things grow!" Maggie told her and turned away to begin her long walk back to her home.

"How long has Maggie been a widow?" Mary asked Cade.

"Oh, Maggie isn't a widow. She's been married to a scumbag for almost ten years. They bought a big old frame house in town and she had plans of filling it with children, then she found out that her husband was a liar, a cheat and a gambler. As far as I know, that's when she threw him into another bedroom and took in boarders to fill all the rooms up. I've known Maggie from the time we were youngsters. We grew up in the same town, and then they moved here, and we renewed our friendship. If I thought it would help, I'd beat the crap out of her husband. But others have tried it, and he hasn't changed one iota. When he bought the house, he had it put in Maggie's name. That way he couldn't gamble it away. The money she brings in from the boarders buys what she needs and all the food it takes to cook for all of them. She's a real nice lady who has a mess of trouble on her that she doesn't deserve."

Mary felt for Maggie's dilemma. She vowed to help her as much as she could. She liked the woman for getting her and Cade together and for holding her head up high no matter how despicable her husband was.

Cade and Mary wondered all over town after that. They watched Chris and Cam compete in the three legged race and win. They saw Kit, Cooper and Cody try and catch a greased pig. They ran all over the pen and finally Cooper just sat down and one pig came and sat on his lap. It was a crazy way to win, but Cooper didn't care! They gathered up the family to go back and eat lunch only to be stopped by the Sheriff and his Deputy.

"Howdy, Cade..." The older one spoke up. He was wearing a shiny badge declaring him to be the Sheriff. He held out his hand to Mary, "I'm Wyatt Tate, Ma'am. I hear you're a working wonders out at the ranch. Jonah's been singing your praises every time he comes in with a new load each Monday."

"Thank you, Sheriff Tate. I'm glad to be here. Cade and I are real happy." She liked the older man, he had grey hair and a growing paunch, but he had friendly eyes. She wasn't so sure about the deputy.

He was looking at her as if...she wasn't wearing any clothes! Mary wanted to slug him! Cade wasn't paying attention, he and the

Sheriff were talking about the crops and if he had any trouble with rustlers.

The deputy held out his hand to shake Mary's and kept holding it in both of his. "I'm real glad you came to Pine City. I like welcoming all the pretty ladies personally. If you ever need...anything...anything at all, you just let Deputy Brody Hudson know."

Mary grabbed her hand away from the Deputy and leaned into Cade. She suddenly felt dirty just for having him shake her hand. In minutes, she and Cade were on their way to the wagon, but she could still feel the deputy's eyes on her as they walked away. He had dulled a rather exciting trip to town.

The family relaxed as they ate the fried chicken and potato salad Mary had made for them. Deviled eggs and berry turnovers completed the lunch they all enjoyed.

"That was sure good, Mary, after all I ate, I'm not so sure that I'll be hungry at dinner!" Cade told her as she carefully packed up all the dishes into the boxes she had brought with her.

"Oh, then you won't mind me giving some of our ham sandwiches away for dinner and the apple pie I made?" Mary teased.

"Not a chance!" Cade told her, "I don't care how full I am, we are not giving away any dessert you make, especially an apple pie!"

The children were in a hurry to go off and play. It was not often that they got to play with other children. Chris and Cam were joining Rose and Dylan Graham to play a game of stick ball. Chris hoped he could talk David Drew into joining them, because as Chris said 'He can hit that ball a mile!'

Kit and the two younger boys were going with Lily Graham and Emma Drew to look at a new batch of puppies that they knew were at the livery. Cade warned them to not stray too far and to come back and check in with them every thirty minutes or so. Kit promised them they would. She was eager to spend some time with her friends; it wasn't often that she had the pleasure of playing with girls. She didn't mind that Cody and Cooper had to tag along with them.

For once, Cade and Mary were alone and allowed to spend some time without any children around. Cade was just getting comfortable with his head in Mary's lap when Diana Scott turned up.

"Cade! It's so good to see you. It's been too long, I've been out several times, but you're never at home, you're always busy doing god knows what at that ranch of yours!" Diana said sitting down very close to Cade without being invited to join them. "It's not often that I ever see you without the little ba...children around. Where ever are they all?"

Cade sat up and moved away from Diana towards Mary. "Diana, my children are not bastards and I resent you ever calling them that. Cate and I were well and truly married when each of them was born. It upset me and my children."

"Who told you I called them bastards?" Diana was mad and immediately turned on Mary, "If your new...wife...said it, it's a lie!"

"Mary never said a thing. It was Cooper who repeated word for word what you said. He's too young to tell such a lie." Cade was not being so nice to Diana now, "You owe Mary an apology in saying that she was a liar and I'll hear it now!"

"Why, Cade, I was just so upset at someone...even little Cooper...saying I said such a thing! I'm sure he was mistaken...I just adore all your children! Aren't I always making cookies for them to eat? And spoiling them shamelessly?" Diana was trying so hard to get Cade's approval back, she was sweating and her hands shook. "Surely, you believe me...I value our...friendship so very much. Cate was one of my dearest friends, and it just distresses me to see so many changes being made to her home. I know that Cate wouldn't like them anymore than I do!"

"Well, it doesn't matter to me if you like them or not!" Cade told her and put an arm around Mary's shoulder. "The rest of the family is thrilled with everything that Mary has done to make our house a real home. I wish Cate could see the difference it makes in our lives, if she could, I know she would approve of how well Mary takes care of all of us, me especially. You are looking at a very happy and contented husband, Diana, any inkling of anything else is false."

He watched as anger, surprise and resolve ran across her facial features. She even tried to backtrack and get Cade to admit that he missed Cate and the way things used to be.

"Let's get something straight, Diana. I loved Cate and we had a good marriage for twelve years and I hated to see her so sick. I will always miss her, but it's time for us all to move on. Cate would have wanted her family to be happy. Mary has done that. She makes me happier than I've ever been. I agree she's not like Cate. But I love her and she loves me, and we have a good marriage. It's the best thing for my family and for us. So butt out of our affairs. If you want to be friends to Mary, that's up to her, but I for one don't want to hear any more talk about what Cate would or wouldn't have liked!" Cade stood up with Mary. He helped her put all the food back into the wagon. "Now if you'll excuse us, Mary and I would like to go and visit with Jonah and Olivia for a while." He tipped his hat and took Mary by the elbow and led her off. Diana all but stomped her feet, she was so angry! This wasn't working out at all as she had planned. But unfortunately Diana wasn't a quitter. If at first you don't succeed, try, try again! She wasn't finished with Mary Murphy yet, not by a long shot!!

CHAPTER 17

Mary and Cade found Jonah and Olivia just closing up their store. They had done a brisk business with all the ranchers being in town, and they had indeed sold all five of Mary's dresses in one day!

"I wish you could work for us full-time, Mary. I know we could sell every one of the dresses you make!" Olivia told her blushing because she was wearing one of the dresses herself!

"I'm glad you're pleased with my work, but I'm pressed to get everything done for Jonah now, what with making us all new winter coats and keeping up with the housework and gardening. I'm about to start canning all the vegetables we're growing, and then I really will be pressed for time!" Mary told her with a grin. "I sure do appreciate Jonah coming out to the ranch to pick everything up and bringing back everything we want and need. I don't know what we'd do without him!"

"One of these days, I'm going to come out and pick everything up instead of Jonah! He talks and raves about all the changes at your ranch. I can't wait to see it for myself!" Liv told them.

"You know Maggie McDonald is going to come out and visit us real soon. Why don't you come with her, as long as Jonah can handle the store? We'd love to have you at least for a little while!" Mary invited her. She was sure that Cade wouldn't mind if she took a few hours to sit and talk with her new friends.

"I'll do it! I can't remember the last time I took off to visit with friends." Suddenly Liv grinned, "As long as you can promise me that I won't have to put up with Diana Scott! That woman makes me madder than a stepped on snake! Jonah knows that I won't tolerate anyone making unkind remarks about someone I like. I rather enjoyed you asking her to help you weed just so she would leave! I laughed and so did Maggie McDonald. We both had to go into the other room of the store, we were laughing so much!"

"Oh, dear! Does everyone know about that? They're all going to think me terribly rude!" Mary was worried.

"No they won't. They all wish they had thought of the excuse when they were stuck with visiting with her!" This time they all laughed, Cade and Jonah included. Cade was glad to know that his gentle little wife could stand up for herself when she needed to. They spent the afternoon visiting with the Clark's, the Graham's and the Drew's. Mary didn't know when she had so much fun or felt so relaxed.

They called their crew together to eat the ham sandwiches that Mary had made and to finish off her potato salad. They all enjoyed the apple pie she had made for dessert. They started playing music at dusk. They had several fiddlers and a few harmonica players. You could tell they had spent many hours practicing and liked what they were doing.

Cade took Mary out for the first dance and didn't want to let her go to anyone else. But Chris and Cam each stole a dance and then Mary danced with Cody and Cooper while Cade danced with Kit. Kit had stars in her eyes dancing with Cade. He came back to Mary then to reclaim her. He was interrupted by Deputy Brody Hudson who had stepped up to dance with his new wife. Cade didn't like it, but he gave Mary over to Brody.

Mary didn't like Brody and she certainly didn't like dancing with him. Brody thought he was charming and didn't see Mary's eyes flashing over his roaming hands. Mary finally had enough and stopped in the middle of the dance floor.

"Deputy Hudson, either you control your hands or I will! I am a married woman, and I won't put up with how you're holding me or where you've let your hands travel!" Then she turned and walked off the dance floor. Brody was hot on her heels.

"Nobody but nobody walks off on me, Mrs. Murphy!" He went to grab for Mary's arm and she swung it around and connected with his cheek. The slap could be heard all over the dance floor. There was sudden silence as all eyes centered on Mary and the Deputy.

"Don't ever touch me again. In fact, I'd be happy if you never talked to me again!" Mary told him between her gritted teeth. After being pawed by the deputy during the dance, she'd be damned if she'd be civil to the man!

"Oh, you'll talk to me all right! You'll get down on your knees and beg me if I want you to!" Brody threatened Mary. Just who did the bitch think she was anyway?

"When Hell freezes over!" Mary told him and turned away and walked over to where Cade stood with a scowl on his face and his arms folded over his chest.

"What happened, Mary?" Cade asked her in a low voice. He could see how upset she was and if that deputy did anything improper, he'd wipe the floor with him.

"He got a little fresh when we were dancing. When I told him I wasn't having any of it, he went to grab my arm and I slapped him and told him to never touch me or talk to me again. He told me that he would have me on my knees begging him if that's what he wanted." Mary told him without any embellishment. "I hope it's the end of it. I certainly don't want to cause a ruckus, Cade. It's getting late; I think we're ready to go home." She put her hand on his arm. But Cade wasn't looking at her, he was staring at Brody. If looks could kill, Brody would already be dead, but then so would Mary, because Brody was giving her a look that would have crushed a lesser woman.

"You get the kids together; I'm going to have a word with the deputy. Nobody manhandles my wife!" Cade told her and walked towards Brody.

Brody was waiting for him. It was almost like he wanted to have Cade come over so he could fight it out with him. Something was bothering the man about Cade and he acted like he couldn't wait to tell Cade all about it. But their conversation was not to be. Sheriff Tate met the two in the middle of the dance floor.

"All right, you two, you're both going to have to calm down and go your separate ways. I won't have our celebration ruined by the two of you. Brody apologize to Cade for not being respectful with his wife while you were dancing with her." The Sheriff wasn't asking he was telling Brody what he was going to do.

"Sorry..." Brody mumbled.

"Stay away from her, Brody, or you'll answer to me. Do you understand?" Cade asked him in a low voice.

"Like I'm scared of a dirt farmer!" Brody told him back. He was itching for a fight. He felt he had the upper hand; he could wipe the floor with the plow-boy!

He didn't consider that Cade was about five inches taller and every ounce on him was muscle. Cade might not be as fast with the hand guns as Brody, but he was deadly accurate with his rifle. His fists alone were almost twice the size of Brody's and he wanted to plant just one of his fists into Brody's smug face. Cade looked at the Sheriff and nodded his head. "Keep him away from my wife, my kids and me, Wyatt. He's been warned."

Then Cade walked off the dance floor. He headed toward his wagon and his family. He wanted to hold Mary and assure her that he knew it wasn't her fault. He also wanted to let her know he would protect her and her honor with his life. She meant the world to him and he'd be damned if some two-bit deputy who thought he was too big for his britches could make her feel bad.

Chris and Cam had gotten the mules hitched and everyone was loaded into the wagon waiting. Mary gave him a tremulous smile and reached out to put her arm through his. She leaned her head onto his shoulder and whispered, "Thank you, Cade. I'm sorry to cause so much trouble."

"You're the prettiest piece of trouble I've ever run across and worth every second. Don't you worry yourself about it. Brody just felt like he could do anything he wanted, and we both put him straight about that. He won't be bothering you anymore." Cade told her and kissed her upturned face with tenderness. But in the back of his mind was the thought that this wasn't the end of it, Brody had a bone to pick and he didn't look the type to back down without a fight. So be it, Cade told himself. I can hold my own with him or anyone else who bothers by family. Bring it on, Brody; if it's a fight you want, then it's a fight you'll get!

CHAPTER 18

Mary was very busy for the next several weeks. Her garden was producing record numbers of vegetables and Mary didn't plan on losing a single green bean, cucumber, or ear of corn. She was picking vegetables as soon as she had the wash done every morning. After it was picked, she had the children in an assembly line helping her. Cooper broke off the ends, Cody broke the beans into two or three pieces and Kit put them in jars. Mary added water and salt and then put them in her copper kettle over the wash stand for fifteen minutes. Then she'd take them out and put them on the porch to cool. When Cade, Chris and Cam came home, they always helped her carry all the canned vegetables downstairs to her cellar.

Mary always fixed large quantities of whatever vegetable that she was canning for dinner. Green beans mixed with butter, a little onion and few pieces of bacon or ham, were delicious! The children and Cade went back for seconds and even thirds. The ends of the green beans were always given to the chickens and when it came time to do the corn, the corn cobs always went to the pigs. Mary was canning so many jars of food, she asked Jonah to bring her another batch of quart and pint jars so she wouldn't run out. She always sent a big bag of fresh green beans, corn on the cob, carrots, beets, or cucumbers with Jonah to give to his wife Olivia and another to Maggie McDonald. Living in town, she wasn't sure they had gardens or access to fresh grown vegetables. If Mary had some to spare, then so would her friends.

In the back of Mary's mind was the altercation with the deputy. She felt he had a bone to pick with Cade or her or both of them. She didn't know what she had done to make him feel that he could treat her with so much disrespect that day on the dance floor. As far as Mary could remember, she had never met the man until the Fourth of July at the celebration. She didn't feel at ease with Cade out in the fields so much, she started carrying around the little derringer that her friends had given her before she left St. Louis. She and the younger children never went into the woods without a rifle and her derringer. She even started carrying around a knife tied to the ankle of her foot.

With the children's help, they were able to find wild grapes in the woods, and Mary spent several afternoons making grape jelly. She bought a bushel of cherries from Jonah and another bushel of peaches at the end of July. She canned them up so they would be eating pies and cobblers all winter long. She even found the time to make peach preserves. She couldn't wait for the apples to come in during September and October. She had already ordered two bushels from Jonah.

She had traded some beets to Elizabeth for some heads of cabbage that she was making into sauerkraut in a large crock in the cellar. She had also traded some peppers to Ava Drew for some peas. Mary remembered why she didn't plant them; it took forever to get enough to fill the jars! But can them she did along with every other thing she planted in the garden. Her cellar was filling up quickly and Mary was proud of the food they would be eating all next year. It would save them a lot on the supplies they would buy in September and October to see them through the winter. Mary was already making a list of what they would need.

She talked it over with Cade one night as they were eating dinner with the family.

"Cade, how much of what you've grown in the fields do you keep and how much do you sell?" Mary asked him as he went back for seconds.

"Well, I've been selling everything I grow. Why do you ask?" He was a little puzzled, why would he keep any of the wheat, corn, or oats?

"Well, I thought you would keep some of the wheat and get it made into flour, so we wouldn't have to buy it. I thought that if we make a corn crib, it would be good to store all your corn in it and feed it to your cattle during the winter when it's hard for them to find any grass to graze on. And then it occurred to me, that since we now have horses, you would be needing oats for them to eat during the winter months. I could also use several large bags of corn if it was made into corn meal and so would the chickens. The rest could all be sold to pay off our bills at the General Store." Mary told him.

Cade was astonished at her logic. She was correct in all her assessments, it would make more sense to save the corn and have flour and corn meal made out of his own crops. The idea of feeding his horses and mules with his own oats made a lot of sense, too. Damn if he wasn't married to a smart woman as well as a pretty one!

"Mary, I love the idea of using our own crops to feed us. Are you sure you know how to make a corn crib to store the corn?"

"Pa, that's a silly question!" Chris told him, "She knows how to build just about anything; she just needs a little man power. She's not weak in the brains, just in the muscle. Ain't that right, Ma?"

"I won't say that I know how to build everything, Chris, but I can usually figure out most things given a little time. With all of us working, Cade, I think we can get it done in a day or two. What do you think?" Mary felt good that Chris said such nice things about her. She loved this family so much, she really felt like they were her own children.

"I say we get it done before we have to start threshing!" Cade told the room at large. All of the children cheered! Working with Cade and Mary was going to be fun. Mama made everything fun!

By now, after dinner school was progressing very well. The older boys could read from the second and third primer and Kit could read from the first. Cody was doing very well with all his letters and his numbers, but was still struggling with putting them together to make words and sentences. Mary had taken the 2" x 2" boards she had bought and cut them into two inch cubes. She spent several afternoons sanding them down, and then she painted the letters of the alphabet on each side of the blocks. She did the same with the numbers. The children loved to take the blocks and make words they remembered how to spell. Cooper just liked building the blocks and knocking them down. But he was content while she was helping the others. Mary hoped that with their horses this time next year they would be able to go to school in town with all their friends. Her goal was to catch them up to where they should be in school, so they wouldn't be embarrassed at being behind the other children. She knew they needed the socialization with the other children to really become responsible, caring adults capable of taking care of themselves and their family. She loved that she was helping them in achieving their goals.

Maggie and Olivia came for the much needed visit. They brought with them the items that Mary had asked for and the extra jars for canning. She had tea ready in minutes and gave them a piece of pie that she had made for dinner that night.

"Mary, this pie is delicious! No wonder Cade and the boys were praising what a good cook you are." Maggie told her as she finished off her piece of pie.

"Thank you, Maggie, I love to cook and to cook for people who really enjoy it, is a blessing. I never feel like I'm not appreciated around here!" Mary responded.

"Has Diana come back to call?" Olivia asked her quietly.

"No, she has not. I think Cade finally got through to her, that she wasn't his friend, she was Cate's and that I may not want her to be mine! Whatever the reason, she hasn't been to see me since before the Fourth of July. Of course, I've been so busy, she could have come and I wouldn't know it!" Mary laughed.

"She's been seen in town on several occasions. She and the deputy are always talking together. I don't trust either one of them farther than I can see them. There's something not quite right about that deputy. He does his duty, but I've caught him giving some of the wives of the ranchers' kind of a sneer. I don't think he holds any of us in very high esteem. I wish Sheriff Tate would get a different deputy." Maggie told them.

"Well, he certainly knows not to come around here!" Mary told them. "Cade spelled it out very clearly to leave him, his wife, his children and his ranch alone or there would be trouble. The Sheriff heard him and nodded his head. I'm hoping that's the last of it."

"So do we, Mary, so do we! I wanted to tell you thank you for all the vegetables you have sent to us! We have more than enough to eat, I've even been able to put some up in jars and can them." Olivia told her smiling.

"I agree, land sakes, girl! You have been more than generous in sharing your garden with us. I wish there was something we could do to pay you back." Maggie added.

"Just be my friends. I miss Lily and Brenda, my friends back in St. Louis, so much. Having the two of you around, makes me feel so much better. You might try and come around a little more often!" Mary told them.

131

"You just might get tired of seeing us, but it's a deal!" Liv told the two of them. "Now I'd better get the butter, eggs and other things back to the General Store before Jonah sends out a search party looking for us. What do you want us to bring you in exchange for the goods next week?"

"I'm starting on Christmas gifts. I don't know the price of things, so just bring me what I can trade for evenly. If I don't get it this week, I'll get it next week. I want two sleds, a chess game, a checkers game and two pocket knives, two sets of marbles, a doll house, a tea set, whittled animals and a small wagon with blocks and two rocking horses. I also want a pocket watch for Cade and bags of oranges, candy and candy canes. Just tell me how many weeks it'll take me to settle up with you, all right?" Mary told them a little embarrassed at how much she was asking for.

"I don't see anything on the list that should cause any problem. I'll let Jonah figure out how many weeks it'll take you to pay it off. It sounds like you're going to have a very Merry Christmas around here!" Olivia told her with a smile.

"Well, I know things have been very tight for Cade and the children for quite some time. I wanted to make this a Christmas to make up for all the others. Am I giving them too much?" Mary asked.

"Lord no!" Maggie told her and came over to hug her. "You are just what they needed to start smiling and laughing again. I'm going to start making five stockings with their names on them for them to put all those oranges and candy in."

"I just may put in a thing or two just to make sure they have everything they could possibly wish for!" Olivia told her with a hug. "You come see us real soon. You'll need to buy winter supplies, clothes for the children for the winter and possibly some more quilts. It gets mighty cold around here in the winter months. I always worry that we won't have enough firewood for the house and the store, but Jonah tells me I worry too much. He always has a couple of the ranchers around here cut him up several cords of wood to help pay off their bill at the General Store. I guess I just have to trust him!"

"Bye Maggie! Bye Olivia! Thanks for coming out and visiting with me today!" Mary and the children waved until they well out of sight. Then they started digging up potatoes and sweet potatoes. All the hills had to be dug up, the potatoes washed and carried down to the cellar for the winter. The only things on Mary's list still to do in the garden were the pumpkins and the popcorn to be picked and shelled.

When the men came in for supper, they first carried down several hundred pounds of potatoes that they had dug up and washed. They filled the bins they had made and they still overflowed onto the floor. They put the remaining potatoes in burlap bags and leaned them against the bins. It had been a very bountiful summer and September was fast approaching.

"We need to make the corn bin tomorrow. We'll be thrashing wheat in a few days, and once we start we don't stop until everything has been harvested and the fields are clear. It'll probably take us the next six weeks to get us, the Drew's and the Graham's done. We all work together to get us finished. That way we don't have to pay anyone to do it. Is tomorrow a good day to make a corn bin?" Cade asked her as he kissed her cheek before he sat down at the table.

"Tomorrow will work out just fine, Cade. But I've been thinking. Should we make the corn bin here up next to the barn, or should we make it out in the field where it will be closer to the cattle?"

"Now that's a good question. Maybe we should make two bins, one here next to the barn and one out by the cattle. Do you think we can do it in two days' time?" Cade asked.

"With all of us working on it, I think it's doable. I just need to fix us all a big breakfast, make some sandwiches and figure out something easy to make for dinner after we spend all day working." Mary smiled and added, "Nothing to it!"

The entire family started laughing. Then they started making a list of what they needed to do to get it done. Cade chuckled, his wife was something else!

CHAPTER 19

As soon as they woke up the next morning, Cade and the older boys went to milk, gather the eggs and clean out the stalls and let the animals enjoy the green grass while it was still so plentiful. Cade planned on using both oxen to drag back the logs they would use to build the corn sheds. Mary and the boys would work on building the frame. The one by the barn would have a door opening up into the inside of the barn. They would have easy access all winter to get food for the animals. The one in the valley where the animals stayed most of the winter would go up between some oak trees to give it some protection against the fierce winds that blew in with the snow and the sleet.

With 2" x 4"'s, Mary and the boys started the frame by the barn, they carried the lumber and held it in place for Mary to hammer in place. They had the frame up in no time. Then Mary and the boys loaded up the wagon to build the frame for the one with the animals in the valley. Mary used the oak trees to help secure the building and actually nailed the 2" x 4" 's to the oak trees for stability. Mary had enough planks to make the roofs of both sheds. Then she had Chris make her shingles, while she put down roofing paper and tar. Cam handed her up the shingles as she needed them and they had the frames and roofs put on by lunch time. Cade had managed to pull up six long logs into the yard to start making the walls.

The one by the barn only needed three walls. Cade started chopping the long logs into ten and twelve foot lengths. He showed

Chris and Cam how to notch the ends so they could lie on top of each other. It took Cade, Chris, Cam and Mary to lift the logs into place. He had enough logs to get all three walls half way up on the shed by the barn before he had to go back with the oxen to get more logs. While he was gone, Mary had the smaller children start chinking between the logs of the walls already done.

When Cade returned with the oxen, he and the boys were able to finish the walls with the help of the oxen lifting the logs to the higher levels. Mary cut the door to the shed from the barn and fashioned a door. She and Kit helped chink the last logs just as the sun was going down. One shed down, one to go! It had been a long day but they had one done at least. While Cade and the boys put the tired oxen up for the night and did the nightly chores, Mary and Kit got dinner on the table and took down the clean clothes from the clotheslines. She threw Cooper and Cody into the tub to get them cleaned up and hoped to get the rest of them washed before it got too late. They had another long day ahead of them tomorrow.

Cooper almost fell asleep at the dinner table and Cade carried him up and put him in bed. A hot bath felt so good after using all their tired muscles all day. Cade was the last one to jump in the bath tub and he didn't stay long. The bed was looking better and better to him especially with Mary beside him.

Morning brought grey stormy clouds and the promise of rain. Cade left right after breakfast to get some logs with the oxen, and the boys did the morning chores. Mary stayed at the cabin until the three little ones got up and had breakfast and then they got into the wagon to go to the other shed in progress. Mary thought she had everything they needed to get it done. She had nails, hammers, axes, a wheelbarrow to mix the mud and clay to chink the logs and a box for their picnic lunch. She didn't want to waste a minute. They were working against the clock and hoped to finish before the skies let loose with pelting rain.

Cade had already brought four logs by the time she and children arrived at the site. They lost no time cutting the logs into the correct length and notching the ends. Again they worked as a team lifting the heavy logs into place leaving a place for the door, Mary would make at the end. Mary carried up wheelbarrows of mud and clay to chink as fast as they safely could while still laying logs as quickly as possible. They ate lunch as they worked, not trusting the rain to hold off much longer. When it did start to rain, it came down gently at first and they kept on working hoping to finish the job before they started threshing. They were able to finish the shed with everything but the door, and Mary promised that she and the three children would finish it tomorrow while they started threshing the wheat. They hurried home wet to the skin, but content that they had made the sheds to hold the corn and possibly some straw and hay for the one in the valley. It would be more convenient to have both kinds of food for the animals where they lived rather than trying to cart it down in four feet of snow.

When they got home, they found they had company, unwanted company at that. Diana Scott and Deputy Brody had been making themselves at home while they were working down in the valley.

"You're a mighty fine cook, Mary Murphy!" The Deputy called out holding a bowl of what was to be their supper, ham and beans. "Where you been? Diana and me have been waiting for almost an hour."

Cade was fuming. Just who did they think they were inviting themselves to their dinner and coming into their home uninvited and certainly unwanted! He lifted the rifle they always carried with them and aimed it at the Deputy. "I want you off my land and out of my house by the time I count three or I'm going to open up and shoot you for trespassing. One...two...three...!" Cade swung the rifle up and shot the ground in front of the Deputy's feet. "That was a warning shot that I mean what I say!"

"Now see here..." Brody yelled, "I got official business and a legitimate reason for being here! The sheriff is going to be mighty angry if his deputy gets shot in the process!"

"State your business and then go! I know that the Sheriff didn't tell you to go into my home when we weren't there and help yourself to our meal. Now speak up and be gone!"

"The Sheriff wanted to know if any of your cattle have come up missing. A few of your neighbors have sent word that there's a cattle rustler in the area. We were just seeing how many cattle we have to look out for." Brody told him with a smug smile. He wasn't leaving until he was ready to leave!

"You've told me. As far as I know, we haven't had any cattle come up missing. We'll check first thing in the morning before we start thrashing. Now get the hell off my property!" Cade raised the rifle again.

Cade was so busy with Brody, he didn't pay any attention to Diana. Diana had been trying to get behind them for some reason. But Mary wasn't in the mood to leave her alone. She pulled the derringer out of her pocket and pointed it at Diana. "What are you up to, Diana? Cade told you we didn't exactly want you around, you're not his friend and you're certainly not mine."

"I can't believe you'd point a gun at me! I was such a good friend to Cate! I came to see her almost daily and gave her my elixir for long health." Diana started to tell them all over again.

Mary had finally heard from Wes about the ingredient Diana was putting in the cookies. "Is that the same elixir that you gave to your beloved husband?" Mary asked softly.

"Why, yes, yes it was!" Diana cooed.

"Your husband dropped dead didn't he from drinking that drink? And then so does Cate...what exactly do you put in your elixir?" Mary asked watching her very closely.

"Why some of my secret ingredients and a sleeping potion...why do you ask? Would you like some to try?"

"No, I'd probably end up dead just like they did!" Mary told her. "Is arsenic one of your secret ingredients? I thought I smelled an almond odor in the cookies that you gave us. I sent some off to my friend in St. Louis. He determined that they had arsenic in them and sprinkled on them. Were you trying to kill all of us?"

"Kill? What's this you say? Are you saying that Diana killed Cate and her husband?" Brody was suddenly very quiet and he was looking at Diana directly.

"A little arsenic is good for the soul...I've been giving some to Howard for a long time, and it didn't kill him. He just had stomach problems..." Diana's voice trailed away.

"Yeah, Cate had stomach problems soon after you came to call that first afternoon after you moved into your new house, just like Howard was having. There are just too many similarities between their two deaths. I don't like coincidences and it just didn't add up." Mary told them watching Brody and Diana.

"Why did you kill Cate?" Brody asked softly.

"Well, I didn't set out to hurt her...But she was married to Cade and he was such a fine figure of a man...Howard was just Howard. I didn't set out to kill her, just to make her sick. I wanted Cade to see her for what she was! A weak cheating wife who lied to her husband every day! I knew the real Cate; she told me all her secrets! I knew about Brody and Cate..." Diana began only to be cut off by Cade.

"There was no Brody and Cate and my wife was not a weak cheating woman! What are you talking about?" Cade asked her in a near shout. He had forgotten about Mary and his children standing right behind him by the wagon, their eyes as round as saucers as they listened to Diana and Brody talk about their mother. She was suddenly a woman they didn't recognize.

139

"You had been blackmailing Cate, hadn't you Brody?" Mary suddenly spoke into the sudden silence. "Did you threaten to harm Cade or her children to get her to do what you wanted?"

"How did you know?" Brody said into the sudden intake of air by Cade.

"You were angry at the Fourth of July dance. You felt that Cade killed Cate for being with you and taking her away from you. I don't know why you selected Cate to threaten, but regardless how she felt about you, you loved her, didn't you?" Mary guessed.

"Yes...I loved her. I had never let any woman get that close to me, but she slipped past all my defenses and before I knew what was happening, I loved her beyond all reason. I met her before she was married to Cade. She told me I'd have to marry her to keep her, I told her I wasn't ready to get married and before I knew it, she was gone and married to Cade! I tried to get her out of my system. I slept with more women then you can think of or even try to count, none of them compared to Cate. I had to find her! We renewed our relationship when I became the deputy. I had to use a little blackmail to get her to resume it, but it was worth it. I hated that she was sick and getting sicker. Now I find out that Diana was the one to take her from me..."Brody confessed.

"I didn't mean to take her from you!" Diana shouted at him! "I just wanted Cade to turn to me out of loneliness! I wanted to be the one he fell in love with! I would have sent those little bastards off to boarding school as soon as I could. Then it would be just Cade and me! It would have been so perfect...and then SHE came along. The perfect little wife and mother to all his children and to Cade, too. It was just too much! All my plans were for naught, I was going to end up with nothing and nobody!" Diana yelled.

Brody didn't stop to blink; he pulled his pistol and fired three times, hitting Diana in the chest. She looked astonished that he would do such a thing to her and then she fell down in a pool of her own blood. She was dead before she hit the ground. The children and Mary screamed!

"Drop the gun, Brody!" Cade told him. His mind was spinning at all he had just heard. It couldn't be true, not his Cate. But it explained so much. How she would cry for long periods of time and when asked why, she would reply that he wouldn't understand. He thought she was in such pain that that was why she cried so much. He remembered encouraging Diana to visit her often to help lift her spirits, but she only got worse and worse until she couldn't even get out of bed in the morning. If she was being poisoned, it would explain the pain but not the crying. If Brody were blackmailing her into doing whatever he wanted her to do, that would explain her words of 'I'm not worthy of you!' and 'I just want to die!' Diana had simply done what she had wanted her to do...help her die.

Brody dropped his guns and stood there while Cade tied him up. He was a broken man. Cade wanted to hit him and beat the holy crap out of him for making Cate feel so unworthy, but he felt he'd leave it to the law for now. He needed time to think.

Mary covered Diana's body with a blanket and the boys helped her lift her lifeless body into the wagon. It was still raining so they parked the wagon inside the barn for the time being. Cam and Chris took the horses of Brody and the horse from Diana's buggy into the barn and gave them food and water. They took Brody into the house. They all took time changing into dry clothes and eating some of the ham and beans that Mary had made for their dinner. Was it only this morning? It certainly seemed like a lot more time had elapsed than only less than an hour. So much had happened in such a short time, Cade didn't think his world would ever be the same again.

CHAPTER 20

Cade walked around the cabin in a state of shock. He couldn't believe what he had just learned from Brody and Diana! He also couldn't believe that Brody had just shot Diana down in cold blood in front of his wife and his children! He couldn't imagine how they were feeling about their mother now after hearing everything that was said. It certainly tarnished the good memories he had had with Cate over the past twelve years.

How could she have acted like such a loving wife while keeping such a secret from him? Was he so blind that he didn't notice another man around the place? Did his children know about Brody and not tell him for fear of how he would react? He had so many questions and really feared what the answers might be. But Cade wasn't a man to beat around the bush. He and Brody were going to have a little talk, man to man if need be. He'd get the answers he needed one way or the other. In the meantime, he would comfort his children and his wife the best way he knew how.

After they had all changed into dry clothing, the Murphy family sat down to dinner with the rest of the ham and beans that Mary had made that very morning. He knew that it was probably mouth watering like everything else she cooked, but to Cade it tasted like sawdust. He was having trouble even swallowing.

Mary looked at his pale face and knew how he must be suffering over what he had just learned. She knew how she would feel if she had learned anything so horrible about her husband, Ben. It would have almost destroyed her to find out such a shocking truth. How could she help Cade get through this? She watched the faces of the five children, they were suffering too. Mary had her work cut out for her that was for sure!

She quietly gathered up all five children and took them up to the loft to get them ready for bed. She wanted them safely tucked into bed before Cade and Brody talked, really talked without the possibility of little ears hearing more than they needed to hear. She kissed all five children and told them that she loved them. They all gave her the hugs and kisses she wanted in return. Chris and Cam had a haunted look about them.

"Boys, if you would like to talk about what was said and done out in the yard today, I'm always going to be here to listen to what you have to say. Sometimes it helps to talk to someone about what's bothering you..." Mary waited for the words to sink in.

"Ma...our first Ma was a good person. But she wasn't strong like you are. She didn't try to change anything, she'd make do and she had us make do. We were happy the way things were. And then one day the deputy came to call." Chris took a deep breath as he was trying to make sense of all that happened.

"Ma started crying a lot then. She didn't feel all that good, but she was getting out of bed each morning and trying to cook and clean for us all. Cooper was just little bitty then and she spent a lot of time feeding and changing him. Chris and me helped her look after Kit and Cody. We were only ten and eight then and not as much help to Pa as we are now. We weren't big enough to cut wood or even to help him weed the crops and brand cattle. Pa was doing everything himself..." Cam told her quietly.

"When did Diana start showing up?" Mary asked them.

"She came right after Cooper was born...but she didn't start coming around a lot until he was about one or so. Crying babies made Diana act weird. Once, Cooper started crying, she'd find some excuse to leave in a hurry!" Chris told her. "We even pinched him a few times to get him to cry just so she would leave!"

Mary smiled picturing the crying baby and an exasperated Diana. "Was she giving your Ma her elixir then?"

"Yeah, but not as often then as she did near the end."

"...Just cookies?" Mary asked them.

"Yeah, but me and Cam didn't like the stomach aches we got when we ate them, so we only pretended to take them and then we threw them away. We watched over the little kids so they wouldn't eat them either. I don't think there were any left by the time Pa came home from the fields." Chris told her.

"When the deputy came to call, Ma usually asked us to go to the barn while they talked. We didn't like him none at all, so we didn't mind leaving them for grown up talk..." Cam looked at Mary with tears in his eyes, "We didn't know what they were doing, honest!"

"I know, Cam, you were just doing what your mother told you to do. None of this is your fault! I'm not so sure that it was your mother's fault either. She was being blackmailed and poisoned at the same time. I'm not so sure that her thinking was all that sound what with being pressured by Brody and Diana, trying to protect Cade and her children from all of it." Mary told them in a low voice. "I do know that she loved Cade and her children very much to go through so much pain. Let your father come to grips with all that's happened, and he'll see for himself that your mother was caught up in a web not of her own making. Now you boys better get some sleep, I've got a feeling we'll all be going into town tomorrow to take the body in and the Deputy." Mary kissed the boys again and left them to think over all that she had said. She hoped that it had helped. Now to be able to do the same thing for Cade.

Cade was sitting in one of the rockers just staring into the fire of the fireplace. His thoughts were such a confused jumble. How could this have happened to Cate? To him? To his family? It just didn't make any sense!

As Mary walked down the stairs, she heard him ask Brody in a low voice, "Did she ever love me? Did she just stay here for twelve years waiting for you to come back and take her away from us?" Mary's heart went out to Cade, his heart was breaking.

"No..." Brody answered him. "It's because of how much she loved you that she was in such a quandary. She loved two men, one she was married to and the other she enjoyed his company very much. She loved you too much to leave you or the children. I should know...I asked her often enough to let me take her away from all this. I wanted to be the one to give her children and care for her. It tore me up to leave her every time knowing that she loved you so much that she wouldn't think of it. Even when she thought she was dying, she wouldn't even consider it."

There was silence for a while and then Brody talked again, "I met Cate while you had gone to put in a claim on land here. You were gone for over two months. During that time, I tried everything in my power to make Cate fall in love with me. Even then she loved two men. She didn't love me enough to go away with me and I didn't love her enough to marry her. I felt I was too young, we both were. I left for a week to give her time to miss me and to think it over, but when I came back, she was gone. You had returned and you'd married her and took her off to Wyoming. I was crushed...I almost came after her, but I decided that I didn't need any woman enough to give up my bachelor status for.

"I must have tried to make every girl I met fall in love with me in the next ten years before I woke up and realized that I was measuring every girl I met with Cate and they were all coming up short. I decided that if I made something of myself, then Cate would see what she had missed. I became a Deputy and I'll admit a good one. I still kept an eye out for the ladies, but it was all for

145

naught. Two years ago, I ran into one of your relatives and he let it slip where you and Cate were living. I took off hoping to find her and a job. I did both.

"The existing deputy had just gotten shot. The job was mine. Now I just had to work on getting the girl. For the longest time, I would sit on the hill overlooking your homestead and watch your whole family through the spyglass I carry with me. But looking wasn't enough; I wanted to feel her in my arms again.

"She wouldn't even talk to me; she ran into the cabin and told me to go away and never come back. I couldn't do that...Diane saw how I felt about Cate and told me she would help me get the woman I loved back. She had designs on getting you when Cate left you. Every time she went to visit Cate, Diana would tell her what a wonderful man I was. How could she have ever chosen you over me? I didn't know that she was slowly poisoning the woman I loved and her husband so she could get what she wanted.

"You were right, Mrs. Murphy, about me blackmailing Cate to get her to see me. I was desperate and willing to try anything. I told Cate that if she didn't start seeing me, I was going to shoot you or one of the children. That was why she started seeing me again...she was scared of losing one of her children or Cade. I didn't care how it got done, I was able to see Cate again and I took the chance over and over again just to be able to spend a few minutes with her.

Brody took a deep breath and looked at Cade. "She never slept with me. I wanted her to, but she never would and then she was too sick for me to even consider it. I was content to just hold her for a few minutes and steal a kiss or two. It wasn't enough, but it was all I had...And then she died. I fell apart. I couldn't eat or sleep. I went through my days in a haze doing whatever they told me to do. And then I saw you drive through town with your new missus. It had to be on the day you got married.

"I started hearing about the new Mrs. Murphy. She was doing all sorts of changes at the homestead. How everyone was so much happier with the new Mrs. Murphy than they were with the old one! I went back to my old hillside and started watching you. You didn't look like Cate and you sure didn't act like Cate...I began to think that maybe Cade got tired of having a sick wife and he got rid of her so he could get a new one. He sure looked a lot happier with the new one than he ever looked with Cate. I was going to make you pay for taking my Cate away from me. I was going to let Diana kill your new wife, so you would know how I felt! It was crazy, I knew I wasn't thinking rationally, but at the time I wanted everyone to hurt as much as I was.

"I don't regret killing the Scott woman. She killed the love of my life and her husband. She deserved to die...But I do regret making you all go through seeing her die and hearing about me and Cate. For what it's worth, I'm sorry." Brody told Cade.

Cade didn't say a word, he just looked at Brody and then he got up and walked to the bedroom and shut the door. Mary followed him. "Cade?" She asked into the darkened room.

"Mary...my Mary, let me hold you for just a little while. So much has happened and I've heard so much, my head is spinning. I don't know what to think anymore. I just know that I love you and with you by my side, we can get through anything."

Mary walked into Cade's arms quickly and for the longest time she just let him hold her. Finally she started talking to Cade in a low voice. "Cade, I know you're going through the entire chaotic event of the Deputy and Diana and Cate over and over again in your mind. I just wanted to let you know that I know that Cate loved you and the children very much...she went through so much pain and agony just to make sure that nothing would happen to any of you. She was being poisoned and in terrible pain, she was also being blackmailed, she was in love with two men at the same time. I'm sure that she was being torn apart feeling disloyal to you spending time with Brody, but she was protecting you, too. He had to blackmail her just to get her to see him again. That has to tell you something...Diana was an evil, manipulating woman. She desired you enough to slowly kill your wife and her husband and she tried to kill your children, too. It was only through the quick thinking of your two oldest boys that they all didn't suffer from the effects of arsenic poisoning." It was here that Mary paused and leaned back to be able to look into Cade's face and eyes to see if he were listening to her words. "Remember that she loved you, Cade and let the rest go..."

"She may have loved me, but not enough. Not enough to trust that I would have done something to keep the Deputy from hurting me, the children or even Cate anymore. I wish she would have confided in me...reached out to me to help me understand why she was hurting so much. Maybe I could have helped, but at least there wouldn't have been any secrets between us." He paused to kiss Mary's forehead, "Please don't ever hesitate to tell me about anything that's bothering you. I couldn't bear to lose you Mary, I love you so much...but then you're different than Cate was. You take charge; you don't let things take charge of you. You would never give in to blackmail, hell; you'd of probably shot him before you let him hurt any of us. I don't see you being so weak to cry about something and not do something to change it. You could never be Diana's friend. She wanted a weak person she could manipulate into doing whatever she suggested, you would have sent her on her way lickety split, like when you had finally had enough and asked her to weed with you! She didn't know how to get to you, so she turned to Brody to get her what she wanted...I can't find it in my heart to feel sorry for her after hearing that she killed Cate and her husband just to get what she wanted."

"Well, I can't fault her for her taste in men. I find I'm very drawn to you too and I love you very much, Cade...Let's take them both into town tomorrow and then try to put it behind us and move on with our lives..." She looked up hopefully into Cade's eyes. He nodded. They made sure the Deputy was settled for the night and went to bed.

They were both up early. Cade slept fitfully and held Mary all through the night. She was his strength. They found the Deputy still asleep just like they had left him. Cade went out to milk and gather the eggs and Mary started breakfast. All their wet clothes had just been thrown onto the back porch last night. Mary started wringing them out to wash them. She had them clean and drying on the lines by the time Cade came in for breakfast. Cam and Chris were awake and dressed for whatever their father wanted them to do.

Cade untied the Deputy to eat and to take him out to the outhouse. Then he retied him and put him in the wagon. Mary got the other children up and dressed and fed. She herded all the children out the door and into the wagon. It was decided that Mary would drive Diana's buggy with her body in it and Cade would drive the wagon with the Deputy and all the children. Mary took their list of supplies they needed and thought they might as well get everything they needed now so they wouldn't have to make another trip into town.

Driving Diana's buggy into town with her dead body in the back caused quite a ruckus, to say the least! Having the Deputy tied up in their wagon didn't help.

The Sheriff came out of his office and took off his hat, "Would someone tell me what in the Sam-hill is going on around here?!"

It was Brody who told him what he had done and why. He didn't leave out the fact that he was blackmailing Cate into seeing him, or that Diana had confessed to poisoning both Cate and Howard, her

149

husband. The entire crowd was in a state of shock. How could this be happening in their quiet little town?

Wyatt Tate pulled himself together and sent someone off to get the undertaker, took Brody into his jail and locked him up and sent Diana's buggy to the livery to be taken care of. He didn't know what to say to Cade or to his family. He finally just shook his head and put his hand on his shoulder and gave him a gentle squeeze.

Cade understood, he was letting him know without saying a word how deeply he felt that any of this had taken place. He nodded his head and then he helped Mary up into the wagon to go to the General Store to get the things on her list. He was a month early, but knew that Jonah would let them add the rest of their supplies on their bill. He would settle up with him at the end of the month when his crops had all been sold.

It was while they were in the General Store that trouble hit again...there had been a shooting at the saloon over a poker game! Maggie's husband had been shot!

CHAPTER 21

They only heard bits and pieces of what had happened in the saloon. Mary looked up at Cade and told him she had to go to see Maggie, she didn't need to be alone at a time like this. Cade agreed. He told her that he would see to the filling of their order and watch all five children and then he would drive to Maggie's house to see how she was doing. He kissed Mary and watched her and Olivia walk out the door and head for Maggie's.

It took them little time at all to reach her house. Olivia didn't even knock; she opened the front door and quietly walked in calling out to Maggie who they were, so they wouldn't startle her. Maggie was sitting on her couch in the parlor. She wasn't saying anything nor was she crying.

"Maggie?" Mary said and sat down beside her on the couch. "What can we do to help you?"

Maggie shook her head in sorrow and looked with bleak eyes at her two friends. "I can't say that I haven't been expecting this day since the time I heard what he really did for a living. When he was courting me, he told me he was an investor and traveled a lot. It was only after we had been married for over a year that I finally knew what he was. All my dreams went up in smoke. I was married to a liar, a cheat-he confessed to sleeping with several women and a gambler. He didn't invest in anything but the best way to con someone out of their money." She looked around at the big house and her first tear slipped from her eye.

"We were going to fill this house up with children. I wanted babies, so many babies that I could love and spoil...but it wasn't to be. The only thing I ever filled this house up with were boarders to help me pay for the taxes and living expenses. Stephen McDonald couldn't be depended on to have money when I needed it. I made him sleep in a room upstairs. He ate some of his meals here, but after learning the truth about him, I refused to have anything to do with him. I've been so lonely even in a house filled with boarders.

"I know what they say about me in town...I'm cold...my husband turned to other women after I turned him out. But it's not true! I loved my husband when we were first married. And then that love turned to hate and distrust. How am I supposed to act now that he's dead? I won't cry over losing him, I lost him over nine years ago. I cried buckets then; I didn't see any way that my world would ever be right again. Maybe it won't...I just don't want to be a hypocrite about my feelings." She paused, "I'm sorry that he died over something as trivial as a poker game, but I'm not sorry he's gone. He's been gone for a long, long time."

Mary hugged her and so did Olivia. "Regardless of how you feel about the man, he was your husband. We need to make the proper arrangements with the undertaker and the preacher. We will need to have a funeral. You don't have to cry and carry on how much you will miss him. But you do need to keep up appearances. You will still be living here in Pine City. People have short memories and will forget what a pitiful husband he really was. You can do this, Mary and I will help you every step of the way. You're not alone, Maggie, let us help you..." Olivia urged.

As if a sudden thought came to Maggie, she turned to Mary. "Is the threshing done? Why are you in town almost a month earlier than when I thought you'd be? What's going on?"

Mary gave a huge sigh. "We had to come in early because...Deputy Brody Hudson shot Diana Scott in our back yard yesterday when he learned that she had poisoned Cate and her own husband, Howard." There were gasps of surprise from both Olivia and Maggie.

"What in the world...why would he do that instead of just arresting her?" Maggie asked.

"It seems that Brody had loved Cate for over twelve years. He had blackmailed her into meeting him ever since he had come to town two years ago. Diana encouraged them, all the while giving poison to Cate and Howard in the form of her famous elixir. She had even put arsenic on the cookies she was giving to the children. She wanted them gone too. Brody had thought that Cade had gotten rid of Cate since she was sick and he wanted a different wife. That's why he was acting so crazy at the Fourth of July picnic and dance. He blamed him for her loss, he loved her beyond all reason it seemed.

"They came over to our house while we were gone and made themselves at home. Cade ordered them off the property and started an argument with Brody. Diana got involved and it came out how she poisoned them. I had some misgivings over her from the start. She was phony and I felt something was wrong. I sent one of her cookies to my friend, Wes Peters, in St. Louis. Wes works as a U.S. Marshall. He had a friend do some kind of analysis on it and it came out that there was arsenic in the cookie and sprinkled on top.

"She confessed to everything and couldn't see where she had done anything wrong. When Brody learned that it was Diana, not Cade who had killed his love, he lost it and shot her three times in the chest. Diana was dead instantly and fell in a pool of blood...Cade feels terribly that something like this could go on and he wouldn't know anything about it. He feels that Cate didn't trust him enough to confide in him. The children are still in shock at witnessing a murder right in front of their eyes and feeling guilty that they should have said something to their father when the Deputy came to call so much. Needless to say, it's been a long night and day. When we told the Sheriff, or rather Brody confessed to the Sheriff, he just gave Cade a handshake and told us, he'd take care of it."

"You poor dears! You've been trying to make me feel better and here you've been going through a traumatic experience of your own! How awful Cade must feel!" Maggie told her and enveloped her in a hug. "He and Cate had been sweethearts for as long as I can remember, he did leave to get the land here...Now that I think about it, I remember seeing Cate with someone else while he was gone. I didn't think anything about it then, it must have been Brody."

"Diana says she was in love with two men at the same time. To her credit, she wouldn't leave Cade or the children. With the poisoning and sneaking around and seeing of Brody, I feel Cate felt like she was in an impossible situation...she was trying to protect her family, but with the poisoning and the pain she was in, I don't think she was thinking very clearly." Mary told them.

"I'm so glad that Cade has you Mary," Olivia told her. "He needs a strong woman to help him and the children get through this." It was at this time that Cade and the children arrived at her door.

Cade held out his arms to Maggie and just said, "I'm sorry more than I can say, Maggs." Maggie walked into his waiting arms and put her head on his shoulder. She gave him a hug in return.

"I'm sorry, too, Cade. I wish I had known everything that Cate was going through. Maybe I could have helped. But with Diana always around, I kind of felt like I was being pushed out as her friend. Just when she needed me the most, I quit going around so much." Maggie told him with sorrow in her voice, "If I would have known about Brody, I would have told you, if that helps at all."

"It does. Mary tells me it's always easier to bear trouble if you share the load with a friend or someone who loves you. It's good to have friends like you and the Clark's, and Mary...has been the salvation of our whole family. My wish when this is all over, Maggie, is for you to find someone like my Mary to share your life with. You're still a young woman; you have a lot of years left to share with someone you love. Don't turn away all men just because Stephen was such a rotten apple."

Maggie didn't tell him she was over with men in general, but she held her silence. Together they climbed into Cade's wagon, and he took them to the undertaker to make arrangements about her husband. Chin up and shoulders back, Maggie did what she had been doing for nine years, she did what had to be done.

The funeral or funerals of Stephen McDonald and Diana Scott were held the very next day. It seemed like the entire town showed up, not because they held Stephen in such high regard, but because they liked and respected Maggie so much. Diana's funeral was more an oddity than anything else. She had few friends, if any and most just came to see what was going on. She was buried next to the husband she murdered. Telegrams were sent to try and notify any existing family that either she or her late husband had.

It seems for once that Stephen was holding a winning hand in the poker game. He had over a hundred dollars in his pockets when he died and it all went to Maggie. Maggie took it gladly. Brody had been one of her boarders and she lost him, the teacher had been one of her boarders and he was leaving to get married, so she lost him, too. Stephen had taken one of her rooms and now he was gone. The only boarder she had left was the Sheriff, and he announced that at the end of the month, he was going to retire and move to Denver to live with his daughter and her family. Maggie was going to have an empty house and no income coming in. She was a little panicked about what she was going to do about money.

Mary telegraphed to her friend Wes Peters if he knew of any retiring U.S. Marshalls he could recommend for their new Sheriff. He promised that he would ask around and let her know. Mary informed Maggie that now that she didn't have any boarders, she could come out and help her can and finish up her garden. She promised that she would send back lots of vegetables that she could fill her pantry with to help her get through the winter. Chris and Cam told her they'd come in and chop wood for her so she'd be warm, and Cade told her he'd bring in enough smoked meat to last her out the winter. By spring, they would come up with a solution to her problems. Not to be left out, Olivia told her that they would hire her to help out in the General Store a couple of days a week so she would be able to buy the supplies she needed. None of them would let her be alone. She had friends. Maggie smiled and said 'yes' to all their plans. She'd keep busy and maybe the new Sheriff and Deputy would need a place to stay when they came. She could only hope that it had to get better.

CHAPTER 22

The next two weeks were filled with the work around the ranch to get ready for the coming winter. Maggie came out every other day to help Mary finish up in her garden. Mary told her to bring out some canning jars so they could can food for her too. Most of the canning had been done and Mary's cellar was full. But there was still plenty of food on the vines in the garden. Mary, Maggie, Kit and Cody and Cooper cleaned the garden of every ear of corn, bean pod, or tomato they could get their hands on. They dug up the remaining beets. Before you knew it, Maggie had over four dozen jars of vegetables canned and ready for storage. She also had several large bags of potatoes, carrots and onions, not to mention some sweet potatoes as well. Mary even sent back a couple of pumpkins for her to cut up and cook down to make pumpkin pies.

Cade and his neighbors, the Graham's and the Drew's, had been threshing the wheat and when he took some of his wheat in to sell, he ended up getting almost five bags of flour milled in the process. He left one at Maggie's house and took the rest home for Mary. He stopped at the General Store and gave Jonah a partial payment on his standing bill. He promised he'd be back to settle up when he got the rest of his crops finished. He saw Maggie helping a customer when he went in, he was glad that she was staying busy and independent.

At the end of two weeks, several surprises happened to make things even better for Maggie. Her sister, Brenda Smith, came to Pine City to see her and she didn't come alone. Wes and Lily Peters came with them. They wanted to see Mary and make sure for themselves that she was as happy as her letters told them she was. Wes was a little concerned about the arsenic and exactly what kind of town they lived in where the Deputy could blackmail someone and no one knew anything about it.

Maggie was ecstatic! She hadn't seen Brenda for years and it was a very tearful reunion between the two sisters. Brenda insisted that Stephen's death was the best thing to happen to her in years. She was free to begin a better life without him. Needless to say, both Brenda and the Peters' stayed at her boarding house. With the Sheriff staying there too, Wes and the Sheriff found lots of time to talk about his job and his Deputy. Wes told him that he would help find a good man to come in and take over the position of Sheriff and his Deputy. It seemed that one of his good friends had just had some bad news. His brother had died and left the care of his daughter to his friend. Sam Kincaid, his co-worker and friend, knew that he couldn't continue to be a U.S. Marshall and travel while still looking after his niece. He had a good friend who was getting on in years and acting as Deputy for Sam would be the perfect combination. Wes promised to stay on in Pine City until Sam could get his niece and their belongings together and still get to Pine City. Wyatt Tate was relieved that someone who knew the law would be taking over his position. He didn't want to leave the City in the lurch, but he was just getting too old to do a good job as acting Sheriff. He still felt bad about the Scott woman and Brody doing everything and he hadn't been any the wiser. It was time he retired, and he felt that Wes was getting them a younger man who could do a much better job.

Maggie was thrilled to have the Peters stay at her boarding house, she didn't want them to pay but she needed their rent to buy enough food to feed them. She was proud, but not stupid. She felt much better about being able to get through the winter with the supplies that the Murphy's had helped her with. She was determined that come the spring; she would be planting the biggest garden she could fit in her backyard. She was even thinking about getting some chickens and a cow. She loved bringing home eggs, butter and milk from Mary's every time she came home. If she had her own chickens and cow, she would have her own and not be so dependent on others. In the meantime, she enjoyed the time she spent with Brenda and Lily. Mary and Olivia came in as often as they could to share their visits. Cam and Chris didn't forget their promise to bring in enough wood to get her through the winter. They had already brought her in four loads of wood all cut and ready to be stacked. That made up almost six cords already. Each time they came with wood, they also brought in smoked meat for her. Thanks to the Murphy's she had a ham, bacon, venison roasts, turkeys and wild hens. She would be able to last for several months on their generosity.

Cade finally finished cutting and threshing his land and the Graham's and Drew's. He had several large bags of corn made into corn meal for his family and his chickens and he dropped off a bag to Maggie as well. The rest of the corn went into his corn sheds and they filled the two sheds to overflowing. His oats went into several large bags and stored into the loft of the barn to feed the horses over the winter, the rest was sold and paid off the rest of his account at the General Store. The straw and hay were all cut and stored in the barn and sheds before the first of the snow began to fall. He and his boys had time to go hunting to help refill their smoke house for the winter. For the first time, Cade felt they were really ready for winter. His house was snug and warm, they had enough stove wood cut to keep even the blizzards at bay, and they had enough food for an army stored in the cellar, smoke house and barn. All his animals had been gathered and led to a sheltered patch of ground near some smaller streams. His cattle would have food and water and when necessary they would get the corn that had been stored. Everything that could have been done was finished. He could finally breathe a sigh of relief that they would be safe to last out the winter in relative comfort.

Mary had been busy as well. Jonah came for the last of the dresses that she would make before spring. It was too hard for Jonah to make the trip in all the snow that usually fell, but he did leave enough material for Mary to make more than ten dresses over the winter months! Mary promised him that she would be sure to have them ready by then plus a lot of soap, butter and eggs! She had paid off all the Christmas gifts she had secretly bought for the family and had them safely hidden away. She had also purchased enough wool and flannel to make warmer clothes for her entire family. She spent every spare minute she had sewing. The boys needed warmer pants and they needed to be longer as well. They were growing like weeds. Her entire tribe needed warm flannel shirts to keep them warm, and she made sure they all had enough long underwear to keep the cold drafts at bay. She even made Kit wear long johns under her dresses, and she did the same!

Cade and the boys butchered all three hogs and a steer at the end of October. Mary was thrilled to have so much pork and beef in her smoke house, and she made sure that Maggie had some, too. She was glad that Maggie was not going to be spending the winter alone. Brenda had gone home to St. Louis and George, but Lily and Wes were still there. Wes was staying until Sam could arrive to take over as Sheriff. In the meantime, they were staying in Maggie's boarding house. Mary invited them all out for Thanksgiving if the roads were passable.

Mary outdid herself! She roasted up two turkeys with dressing, mashed potatoes, sweet potatoes with brown sugar and cinnamon, corn, green beans, freshly made sweet rolls, butter and strawberry preserves. It smelled even better than it looked! Maggie and Lily promised to bring the pies, if Mary would whip up some whipped cream to put on top. They didn't disappoint! Maggie had made two pumpkin pies and Lily had made an apple and a peach pie.

It was a very happy crowd that sat down to dinner on Thanksgiving Day. Wes had rented a sleigh to get them out to the homestead. While they were there, they decided to open up the Christmas presents they had for each other because they had doubts that the roads would still be passable by the end of December. Mary had made warm shawls for Lily and Maggie and had made Wes a sweater vest to help keep him warm on his rounds. They had stockings for all the children filled with oranges, peppermint sticks and candy. For Mary, Lily and Maggie had made her a dress. They knew that Mary could sew better than either one of them, but knew she always put herself last and she wouldn't make herself a dress until she had all her children and Cade done. It was a blue that matched the color of Cade's eyes. Mary loved it! For Cade they had a new pipe complete with three different kinds of tobacco for him to try out.

It was a wonderful holiday for them all, but before they left, Mary had one more surprise for them all. She was pregnant and she was due in June. Pandemonium broke out when she announced the coming event. Her children were thrilled; they would love to have a baby around the house again. Cade was so pleased that he could give Mary her wish, to be able to hold another baby in her arms. Maggie's eyes misted over. She was so happy for Mary and Cade, and secretly wished that she could hold a baby someday, her baby. Wes and Lily looked at each other and they announced that they too would be having a baby in early May. Such a wonderful thing to be happening to two of her closest friends, Maggie felt blessed to be able to share in their joy.

December brought snow, snow and more snow. Mary helped Cade make some snowshoes for himself and the two oldest boys so they would be able to check on the cattle and take care of the other animals on the ranch. Cade even made the trip into town on the back of Big Red to get enough flannel and yarn for several babies. He also ordered a cradle that he would pick up in the spring when they came in for their supplies. In his pocket was his Christmas gift to Mary. When they had gotten married, he had never given her a wedding ring. On Christmas, he would give her the ring and all the flannel he had bought. He couldn't wait to put it on her finger.

CHAPTER 23

Mary made Cade and the older boys chop down a small fir tree to be used as their Christmas tree. She helped the three younger children string popcorn and cranberries to put on the tree. She also cut the tops and bottoms of the tin cans they had used over the past few months into stars that they could hang on the tree. She and Kit also made gingerbread men and they could hang them on the tree. It would not only look good, their tree would smell really good!

The children were really excited about having a tree for Christmas. The last few years with Cate feeling so poorly, they hadn't really celebrated Christmas with the children. They didn't expect presents; they didn't expect anything at all other than Mary making another really good dinner for them to eat. Mary and Cade had put the children to bed early so they would have time to wrap and put their gifts under the tree. They were so happy to be able to give something back to their hard working children after all they had been through. Mary was so excited that she could hardly sleep. She couldn't wait to see their faces when they looked under the tree on Christmas morning.

She was not disappointed! They couldn't believe all that they had under the tree. Mary had put the flannel shirts that she made for them and their new, longer pants under the tree, too. The children weren't used to getting new clothes EVER! Chris and Cam couldn't believe the sleds, marbles, chess and checker sets they received. Kit couldn't get over the doll her new Ma had made for her and a dollhouse with a lot of little furniture and little people to play with. She might even start liking being a girl! Cody and Cooper climbed on their rocking horses and acted like they were riding to California! They loved their little wagon and all the blocks and animals they had to play with, but the horses were their favorite.

Then it was Cade's turn from Mary. She gave him two new shirts, a pair of pants, some Bay Rum and his pocket watch. On the back of the watch, Mary had them engrave the branding iron sign, a large C with an M inside the C and the words, 'All my love, Mary'. He couldn't believe it! He kissed her about five times and kept taking it out and checking the time.

Cade couldn't wait another minute to give Mary her gifts. He got down on bended knee and placed her wedding ring on her third finger of her left hand. "Now nothing can break us apart...I love you Mary with all my heart!" Mary started crying she was so happy and felt so complete. And then he gave her the large bundle of flannel. Enough white flannel to make at least five dozen diapers and enough pastel blue, yellow, green and even some pink flannel to make some sleepers and rompers for the baby to wear. There was also enough yarn to make them all booties! Mary was thrilled; she would have everything done long before the baby was born. Then Cade told her he had one other gift to give to her, but it wouldn't be ready until the spring. He told her that Jonah was ordering them a cradle to use and it would be here in plenty of time before the baby made its entrance.

Mary just kissed him and held onto him crying into his chest, "I'm just so happy, Cade! How could you get all this stuff and I wouldn't even know about it?"

"You had worked so hard to give us all such a special Christmas, I couldn't let the opportunity go by to not make it as special for you as it was for us." Cade stopped and took a deep breath. "When I think of how low we all were last year this time...it's hard to believe that it could be so wonderful now. Telling Maggie that I still needed a wife was the smartest thing I ever did. Are we ever glad you came all the way to Wyoming to meet us and make us a family again! It's like we're living in another world now. We've never been warmer or dressed so well. We've never eaten so good or so much. When we go to sleep, we fall asleep on soft mattresses on beds that are covered with blankets and quilts and we're all snuggly warm. Rain doesn't fall through the holes in the roof, and the wind doesn't blow through the cracks in the walls. We have a wooden floor and a walk in cellar that holds enough food to feed us all really well throughout the long winter ahead. We are the proud owners of chickens, a cow, three horses and two oxen and two mules. They're all secure in warm stalls in the barn and it doesn't leak or have the wind blow through either. I'm not mentioning that we don't owe anyone anything thanks to all the trading you did this spring, summer and fall with Jonah.

"We can expect lots of new additions this spring and summer. Both mares are expecting, as is Belle. I've already made arrangements to have several piglets brought over as soon as it's warm enough. My herd of about four-hundred and fifty cattle will grow to at least six hundred by the spring. And most important of all, we'll have an addition of our own. I can hardly wait to hold the newest Murphy in my arms. It's been a long time since I rocked one of my children to sleep. And all of this is because of you Mary...You gave us hope and love and taught us that there's always another day that's even better than this one waiting for each of us."

Each of the children tried to get into the circle around Mary. She was their light. She was the one who made each of them better than they were before. She loved them unconditionally and gave them all hope that each day was a new day...Don't waste a minute of it! Mary felt so blessed that she had found such a wonderful place to spend the rest of her life surrounded with people who loved her and made her feel worthy. She couldn't wait for spring to get here so she could add one more little person to their wonderful family.

'Ben, Cate, Benji,' Mary thought into the crowded room, 'I hope you're looking down on us and know how much we love you and how much we love the blessings you've given us. Thank you for giving us all another chance at happiness. Thank you for giving us another day to love.'

The End

Note from the Author

I want to personally thank you for your time and effort in the reading of this book. I love writing, and I owe it to my readers to do the best I can. The best source of input to influence my future efforts is your feedback. Please take just a few minutes to share whatever thoughts you may have on this book by going to https://www.amazon.com/author/m_dipaolo and submit a rating and, if you wish, some comments as well. I would really appreciate it.

ABOUT THE AUTHOR

Marcella (Marky) DiPaolo was raised as a farm girl in Moro, Illinois. She was one of six children, and they all interacted daily with their loving parents and grandparents who served as ideal role models for them as they grew up on the farm. Upon graduating from high school, Marcella started her career in business. She also went to college, initially to become an accountant. It was in the business world that she met the person with whom she wanted to share the rest of her life.

It didn't take long for the young couple to start filling up their home with children. It was in the raising of her own that she realized that working with kids was her passion. She decided that teaching was the direction she wanted to go. During the early years, she was the one that stayed home to watch the kids while her husband worked during the day and went to school at night to complete his education. Once finished, he spent his evenings with the children, so she could go on and complete her BA in Elementary Education and later getting a Masters with a concentration in mathematics.

After more than thirty-five years of teaching, she recently retired but continues to teach from time to time as a substitute at a local parochial school. Over the years, Mrs. D., as she is referred to by her students, was recognized for her teaching accomplishments having received several awards and other forms of recognition. 'Mrs. D' has certainly had a very special effect on a lot of young people, all of whom she still considers members of her 'extended' family.

Marcella has a lot of other interests as well. In addition to a voracious appetite for romantic plots and characters, she is also fond of adventure stories and mysteries. She also loves to watch sports, play golf, eat chocolate, and spend as much time as possible with her family.

Marcella's love of reading began at a very early age. However, she never dreamed she might become a writer until much later in life. Being somewhat addicted to historical romances, both in books and on the screen, she has been exposed to a lot of writing styles. This experience and her time on the farm, raising a family, and all those years in the classroom have provided her with a wealth of ideas to apply to her writing career.

Other Books Written by Marcella DiPaolo

Clear Water Bride Series
    Bargain Bride
    Troubled Bride
    Forgotten Bride
    Reluctant Bride
    Runaway Bride

Morgan Brothers Storm Series
    Above the Storm
    After the Storm
    Beyond the Storm

SERIES OVERVIEW

TAKING A CHANCE

Mary Williams has lost her husband, her young son, and both parents in less than a year. She is constantly haunted by the memories of all that she has lost. She decides she needs to leave St. Louis and start over somewhere new, someplace where she can make a difference.

Cade Murphy lost his wife of twelve years a few months ago. He's left with five children and a ranch to take care of. He can't do it all alone. He sends away for a mail order bride, but not too many women want five children when they tie the knot. If Cade doesn't find a wife pretty soon, he may lose the ranch he and his late wife spent years building. He can't spend all his time planting crops and looking after all his children.

One of Cade's friends in Pine City, Wyoming is Maggie McDonald. Maggie has a sister, Brenda, in St. Louis and she just happens to know Mary Williams and her situation. The two sisters decide to play matchmaker. When Cade finds out about Mary from Maggie, he jumps at the chance that might turn out to be the first good thing to happen to his family in many months.

Mary decides to plunge ahead and help him and his motherless children. They both decide that the marriage will be in name only. They both loved their spouses and don't want a real marriage. Time and circumstances will decide their future happiness. Will they both find a new love to change both their lives and that of his five children forever? It could be Taking a Chance for all of them.

A SECOND CHANCE

Maggie McDonald married what she thought was the man of her dreams ten years ago. They bought a house with lots of rooms that she wanted to fill up with lots of children. By the end of their first year of marriage, Maggie finds out that Stephen, her husband, is not the man she thought he was. He's a gambler, a con man, and a cheat. Maggie throws him out of her bedroom and turns her huge home into a boarding house. Later Stephen gets shot over a poker game.

For various reasons, Maggie loses all her boarders and then gets to start over with new and different boarders. They were different because, unlike the former renters that she barely knew, she became closer and more involved in the lives of her new tenants. For example, the new Sheriff, his niece, and his deputy move into her boarding house. They open up a whole new world for Maggie and the new life she wants to have.

Sam Kincaid has been a U.S. Marshall for over fifteen years, recently his brother died in a fire. His niece was one of the few survivors. He needs a stable home for his niece to grow up in. Mrs. McDonald seems to be just the person for Andie, his niece, to get to know.

Maggie's new boarders feel more like family than strangers, and soon a new relationship grows between Sam and Maggie. A Second Chance brings all sorts of surprises to Maggie's Boarding House, and shows her that she should never give up on her dreams.